DO
THE

DOCTOR WHO
THE PESCATONS

Based on the Argo LP record written by Victor Pemberton
by arrangement with the British Broadcasting Corporation

VICTOR PEMBERTON

No. 153 in the
Target Doctor Who Library

TARGET

First published in Great Britain 1991
By Target Books
An imprint of Virgin Publishing
338 Ladbroke Grove
London W10 5AH

Doctor Who and the Pescatons (Argo/Decca ZSW 564) was
first released by Decca Rcords in 1976
The role of the Doctor was played by Tom Baker

Typeset by Type Out, London SW16 1LB
Printed and Bound in Great Britain by
Cox & Wyman Ltd, Reading, Berks

ISBN 0 426 20353 4

1

THE DARKEST NIGHT

The surface of the long, dark river was dancing with tiny
lights. Trillions upon trillions of them, all reflected from a
cloudless sky above, most of them quite content to remain
settled and calm, but others restless and constantly shooting
across the galaxies to leave a long fuzzy tail, which quickly
disappeared with the wink of an eye. Out of this pande-
monium there suddenly appeared one particular light, at first
tiny and indistinguishable from all the rest. But gradually
it grew in size, and by the time it reached the stratosphere
it was a massive ball of fire, tearing its way towards Earth
at an alarming, aggressive speed.

The dazzling meteorite dropped with a thump into a wide
stretch of the Estuary. For a few moments the surface of the
water seethed as though boiling, sending out great whirlpool
shapes until the meteorite finally settled on the seabed below.
Soon, however, the water was calm again, its surface smooth
but for the ripples stirred up by a slight oncoming breeze.
And high above, all was still again, as dark, ominous clouds
turned the evening into the darkest night of the year.

The TARDIS made an uncomfortable landing. It was as

though it had been plucked from space by some vast magnetic force, and pulled down without mercy on to some bleak, unknown resting place. The Doctor had no idea where, or in which period of time he and Sarah Jane had come to. But as the door of the TARDIS opened, and they peered out cautiously into a blanket of darkness, it soon became clear that they had materialized on to an isolated stretch of beach, which seemed to be a long way from the lights of habitation in the far distance.

It was a warm, almost humid night, which seemed to be begging for even the suggestion of a breeze. Everything was so still and quiet, for even the oncoming tide was making no more that a gentle lapping sound on the shingly beach. But, as the crescent-shaped moon slowly popped in and out of high-drifting night clouds, the Doctor and his companion could just make out deep mudbanks all around them, stretching for as far as the eye could see.

'Where are we, Doctor?' Sarah Jane made quite sure she was not going to follow the Doctor out on to the beach until he thought it was safe to do so. 'Can you see anything?'

The Doctor was already out on the sand looking around apprehensively. 'Not much. But it's the British Isles all right.' He stooped down, picked up a large pebble, and felt it delicately with his fingers. 'East coast somewhere, I'd say. Maybe a bit further south. Could be a river estuary.'

'A river estuary? D'you mean the Thames?'

The Doctor threw down the pebble and stood up. 'Feels like it. And yet. .' Without thinking, he unwound his long woollen scarf from around his neck. 'It's a bit warm for England.'

Sarah Jane agreed. As she wiped her face with her hand, she could feel moisture on it. 'Maybe they're having a hot summer. It does happen occasionally, you know.'

The Doctor moved off a few yards and pushed his hat to the back of his head, his eyes picking out the sulphur street lights of a coastal road in the distance. 'It's England all right,' he said confidently. 'Mid-1970's is my guess.'

After a moment, Sarah Jane ventured out of the TARDIS,

but made quite sure she kept close to her friend and companion. 'We didn't choose to come here, Doctor. What happened?'

'I don't know.' The Doctor said no more than that. Sarah Jane frowned; she always knew that when the Doctor didn't have an immediate explanation for a problem, something was wrong.

A few minutes later, they made their way cautiously along the beach, their footsteps crunching on the rough shingle. On the other side of the Estuary they could see distant lights twinkling in the dark, some white, some yellow, some of them moving car headlights, others from houses or bungalows or blocks of flats.

The sign of human habitation, thought the Doctor, was never far away in the twentieth century.

And further still, far to the left of them out at sea, there were more lights, this time draped across the masts and bows of ships passing up and down the English Channel, or into the Estuary itself on their way up the River Thames, heading for the very heart of London itself.

The Doctor stopped walking for a moment. Then he took his hat off and brushed some of his curly hair away from his eyes. 'It's all wrong,' he said suddenly and, to Sarah Jane, quite incomprehensibly. 'We've been brought here for a reason, and yet – and yet... it's all wrong.'

Sarah Jane swallowed hard. She always hated it when the Doctor got serious like this, and it made her very nervous. She moved closer to him, and looked around. 'It's nothing but a beach, Doctor. And what I can see of it, rather a boring one.'

The Doctor didn't answer. His eyes were still scanning the dark horizon out at sea, and the shoreline all along the Estuary. Although there was no sign of life for miles around, his instinct told them that they were not alone. He put his hat on again, and wiped his mouth on the back of his hand – pointlessly, for his lips were quite dry. He moved off again. Sarah Jane quickly followed him, this time holding on to his arm.

3

Further along the beach they arrived at a long row of beach chalets, obviously in demand during this hot spell. But during the night they were unoccupied, so the Doctor and Sarah Jane peered inquisitively through some of the windows. It was only at this moment that Sarah Jane noticed a strong fishy smell. At first she ignored it, imagining that the holiday-makers had been living on fish lunches every day. But then the smell seemed overpowering, and made her feel sick. 'This is enough to put you off fish and chips for the rest of your life!' she sniffed, covering her nose and mouth with one hand.

The Doctor didn't know what she was talking about, for despite his many extrasensory powers, his nostrils always took a little time to detect any alien smells. But as Sarah Jane spoke, he gradually became aware of the strong taste of salt in his mouth, and this was followed by an approaching heat, as though they were moving close to a bonfire.

'How disgusting!' Whilst leaning on the hand-rail of one of the verandahs, Sarah Jane's hand had touched some sticky substance, rather like gum or glue. 'These chalets are covered in muck. I've got it all over my hand – and my shoes!'

'Quiet, Sarah Jane!' The Doctor turned with a start, his voice low but intense.

Sarah Jane froze. Her lovely large eyes were transfixed on the darkness spread out before them. 'What is it, Doctor?' she whispered nervously, hardly daring to speak.

'We're not alone, Sarah Jane.'

Sarah Jane grabbed the Doctor's arm, and held on to it. She could hear her own heart thumping faster and faster. 'What is it, Doctor?' Her voice was barely audible.

'Ssh! Keep absolutely still.'

To Sarah Jane, the seconds seemed like hours as she stood there in the dark, holding on to the Doctor's arm, anticipating she knew not what. As always, the Doctor's hearing abilities were far in advance of her own, and, like a dog, he could make out sounds long before they were obvious to any human being. But gradually, Sarah Jane became aware of the sound. It was really a vibration to start with; she could feel the sensation in her feet, as though there were earth tremors

4

beneath her. The vibration built in intensity, and soon she found difficulty in staying on her feet. Then, accompanied by an even stronger smell of fish, came a hissing sound, like a jungle cat stalking its prey.

Sarah Jane was finding the approach of some alien unknown force too much to take. 'What is it, Doctor? Let's get out of here!'

'Stay where you are, Sarah Jane!' The Doctor threw his arms around her, and held on to her. 'Whatever you do – don't move!'

Almost as he spoke, an all-engulfing green light emerged from behind the beach chalets, casting a sinister green glow over the cowering Doctor and his companion. And then they saw it, slithering its way towards them in the dark, eyes glaring like giant emeralds. It was a huge, towering creature, over twelve feet tall, half-human, half-fish, with shining silvery scales covering its sticky body, and hands like talons with sharp nails, and webbed feet which were veined in red, heavy and clumsy. Its face was weird, almost gothic; it was like a gremlin, a manifestation of the Devil itself.

Sarah Jane could contain herself no more. 'Doctor!' she yelled, as the towering Creature lurched aggressively towards them, its silvery scales pulsating with every thump of its heartbeat. But the Doctor stood his ground. His eyes were staring in awed fascination at the approaching menace, as though hypnotized by the penetrating emerald glow of the creature's eyes. 'Doctor!' Sarah Jane yelled out again, but this time she twisted the Doctor's scarf around his neck, and virtually yanked him back along the beach.

The Doctor and Sarah Jane ran as fast as their legs would carry them over the treacherous shingles. Behind them they could hear the hiss and roar of the fishlike creature, frustrated by its failure to keep up with its prey. But suddenly, the attacking sounds stopped abruptly, and when they felt it safe to do so, the Doctor and Sarah Jane, utterly breathless, paused by the water's edge to look back. To their astonishment, the creature had disappeared. There was no sign of it anywhere along the beach at all.

Out in the middle of the Estuary, however, a vast green glow was reflected on the surface of the water, which was swelling furiously where it had just been so violently disturbed.

The last time the Doctor had observed Earth on his monitor from beyond the galaxies, he suspected that the landscapes and great oceans were looking strangely different from the way they were during that long period of the planet's evolution. The vast deserts of the great continents of America, Africa, and Asia had seemed more pallid than before, the green fields of England and the tropical rain forests from South America to Sri Lanka and Borneo were no longer lush, the mighty Pacific, Atlantic, and Indian oceans were less rich in colour, and the North and South Poles of the planet were, as far as the Doctor remembered, diminished. Yes, since his last visit, something had definitely been happening to planet Earth, and the Doctor wanted to know why.

As soon as the sun rose the following morning, the Doctor and Sarah Jane quickly discovered that their travels had indeed brought them to the middle of the seventh decade of the twentieth century. It was midsummer, and uncharacteristically hot for the sunbathers who had turned out in force onto the beach at Southend-on-Sea in Essex, on the southeast coast of England.

The Doctor and Sarah Jane strolled along the promenade, savouring the heady smells of delectable holiday cooking coming from the small seaside cafés and amusement arcades: sausage and mash competing with candy floss, stewed eels, ice cream, Southend rock, and hamburgers. Everyone looked very happy in their absurd *Kiss Me Quick!* hats and T-shirts illustrated with pictures of pop groups like The Monkees and The Rolling Stones. For those who were not on holiday, however, it was a different picture.

'Some people must live like pigs!'

The Doctor and Sarah Jane stopped abruptly. An aged local council worker was grumbling angrily to himself as he tried in vain to clean up the sticky mess that trailed along the

6

paving stones for almost the entire length of the promenade.

'Kids! That's what it is. Their muvvers let 'em do anythin' they want these days. A good cuff round the ear-hole, that's what I'd give 'em!'

The Doctor exchanged an anxious glance with Sarah Jane, then stooped down to inspect the gumlike substance that was not only fouling the promenade, but also sticking to the sandals and shoes of anyone stepping into it. 'It's the same stuff all right,' he said, half to himself, dipping his finger into the substance. Then he looked up at the old grumbler and asked, 'How much of it is there? Where does it start from?'

'I was told it goes right back on to the beach, down to Westcliff.'

'Westcliff!' Sarah Jane turned to look back along the vast stretch of shingly beach from where they had just come. 'That must be more than a couple of miles away.'

'It's the day-trippers, y'see.' The old grumbler was trying to clean up the sticky mess with a pail of detergent and a hard broom. 'Couldn't care less for the folk who has to live 'ere.' Using an old ice-cream tub, the Doctor collected a sample of the sticky substance which he wanted to analyze as soon as possible. A short while later, he and Sarah Jane were hurrying back to the TARDIS.

'Doctor – look!' Sarah Jane stared in chilled horror. As they arrived on the secluded part of the beach where they had landed, they were stunned to find the TARDIS covered in a thick mass of the green sticky substance emitted by the giant fish-creature. And embedded into that substance were shingles, dead fish and minute crustaceans, and thousands of tiny empty seashells.

The Doctor now knew his adversary. He also knew that for one reason or another, he was not to be allowed to return to the TARDIS.

The Essex Coastal Protection Unit (ECPU) was one of many set up by the Department of the Environment. Its main function was to keep a constant watch for any signs of serious pollution which might endanger the many species of wild and marine life along the Essex coastline. The building was an old converted Army observation look-out post situated on an elevated position near Shoeburyness. From here, Mike Ridgewell and his team could keep a constant watch on shipping passing into the Estuary on its way to London. It could also monitor any rogue ship that decided to clean out its oil tanks illegally in British territorial waters, therefore polluting the coastline.

When the Doctor and Sarah Jane arrived, the ECPU was tackling yet another environmental hazard. But this one was totally unexpected.

'The water is contaminated for about a five mile radius between Westcliff and Shoeburyness.' Mike was poring over the scientific report he had just received by radiophone from the ECPU's research vessel moored just a mile out in the Estuary. Although Mike looked younger than his twenty-eight years, he had a great air of authority, and was greatly respected by the other members of his team, including his long time girlfriend, Helen Briggs. 'What the hell's going on out there?' he snapped, angrily throwing down the report on to his desk.

Helen took off her fashionably shaped spectacles and picked up the report. 'What kind of contamination?'

'I haven't the faintest idea. They're checking it now.'

'It's radioactive,' the Doctor's voice called from the open door of Mike's office. 'That whole area is highly contaminated with radioactivity.'

Mike swung with a start. 'Who the hell are you?'

The Doctor came into the office, and offered his hand for Mike to shake. 'Just call me Doctor.'

Mike shook hands, but was puzzled. 'Doctor who?'

The Doctor grinned. 'Well – if you insist.' Then he turned to introduce Sarah Jane, who had followed him into the room. 'My assistant, Sarah Jane.'

Helen stepped forward and questioned him suspiciously. 'How do you know the water is contaminated with radio-activity? Have you anything to do with it?'

'Not exactly,' replied the Doctor, who was busily inspecting the large wall charts of the Essex coastline. 'But I do have a certain interest in the matter.'

Sarah Jane looked out through the large window at the Thames Estuary stretched out before them. 'Why are there so many boats out there?' she asked. 'It's like an Armada.'

'Where've you been for the past month?' quipped Helen sarcastically. 'In outer space?'

'Something like that.' The Doctor joined Helen at the window. 'What are they looking for?'

Mike also turned to look out of the window. He ran an anxious hand through his shoulder-length blond hair, leaving the midday sun to highlight his tired and strained baby-face. 'It's been like that ever since that meteorite came down.'

Now it was the Doctor's turn to swing back an anxious glance. 'Meteorite?'

Helen was even more suspicious. 'You haven't heard anything about the meteorite that came down into the Estuary?'

The Doctor was cautious in his reply. 'My assistant and I have been travelling – in some rather remote parts.'

Mike continued the story. 'Came down one night during the spring. Caused one hell of a mess – right along the river up to London. There was flooding from here to Windsor. They even had to mop up at the Tower of London.'

The Doctor now turned his attention to another map on the wall. It was of the River Thames. 'What did this meteor look like?'

'Nobody knows. All they remember was a blinding white flash, and the thing just disappeared into the Estuary out there.'

'But you have a fixed position on where it came down?'

'Of course.' Mike went across to the wall map, and indicated to the Doctor the meteorite's exact point of impact in the Estuary. 'Just here.'

'But it must have made a huge crater on the seabed,' suggested Sarah Jane. 'Hasn't anyone been down to investigate?'

9

Mike and Helen exchanged a curious look. 'Yes, they have,' replied Mike in a grave, barely audible voice. He turned away from the wall map, then, looking absolutely miserable, sat at his desk and leant back, his hands clasped behind his head.

The Doctor and Sarah Jane exchanged puzzled looks, which Helen noticed. So it was left to her to explain, she thought. 'The Department sent down a diving team within twenty-four hours of the meteorite's landing. We had two members of our own CPU with them.'

'Yes?' The Doctor's instinct told him what was to come.

'Five men and three women. They were lost without trace.'

'What!' Sarah Jane was horrified. 'You mean, there was an accident?'

'Don't talk crap,' snapped Mike, who leapt up from his desk, and glared tensely out of the window. 'Every one of them was expert in deep-sea diving.'

The Doctor scratched his chin absently. He was clearly thinking hard. 'But you must have been in radio contact with them during the dive?'

'Of course we were,' Helen replied, quickly lighting a cigarette. 'Video contact too. They just cut off. The Navy sent down a specialized diving team later, but found absolutely nothing. No sign of a meteorite – or our diving team.'

Sarah Jane perched herself on a chair by the window and looked out. 'But surely they couldn't have just disappeared like that. I hate to sound indelicate, but by now they must have found bodies or something?'

The Doctor glared at Sarah Jane, who immediately wished she hadn't said such a tactless thing.

Mike swung round on his chair to look aimlessly out of the window again. 'The bed of that Estuary is full of mud. Whatever's left of them, that's where they are.'

'What d'you mean, whatever's left of them?' asked the Doctor curiously.

Much to Mike's irritation, Helen blew smoke from her cigarette in his direction, and he quickly fanned it away. Then

Helen coughed as she tried to speak. 'Some of us think the diving team may have been attacked by a big fish.'

'Big fish?' Sarah shot a quick look at the Doctor.

'There have been sightings of a shark or even a whale.' Helen was still spluttering from inhaling too much smoke. 'It could have come in with the warm weather.'

The Doctor felt he had no need to hear any more. The fish-creature who tried to attack him and Sarah Jane the night before was clearly the big fish Helen was talking about. 'You know, I'm afraid you're not going to get very far until you find that meteorite.'

Mike swung round angrily on his chair. 'I'm aware of that, Doctor – whatever your name is! Since you appear to be so knowledgeable, perhaps you'd care to tell me how we do it?'

The Doctor leaned both hands on the desk, and stared straight at Mike. 'I shall go down to the seabed and take a look for myself.'

'Doctor – no!' Sarah Jane rushed straight across to him. She could see that wilful look on the Doctor's face.

'You?' Helen stubbed out her cigarette in a pencil-tin which she took out of her jeans pocket. 'What do *you* know about deep-sea diving?'

'Not much,' snorted the Doctor. 'But I do know something about marine life. I suppose you could say that in my time I've had some rather interesting encounters with quite a lot of rare large fish.'

Mike and Helen exchanged a look, and he got up from his desk. 'That's all very well,' he said sceptically. 'But what do you know about meteorites?'

The Doctor grinned knowingly. 'Well,' he said, 'I have studied the stars from time to time.'

The mouth of the Estuary was cluttered with small ships of every shape and size. Some of them were small cargo vessels passing back and forth between the English Channel and the Pool of London, and others were sailing boats containing holiday-makers taking advantage of the first breeze of the day. But in mid-Estuary, somewhere between the coasts of Essex

11

and Kent, several small motor launches were gathered together in a small group. On board one of them, which was flying a flag with the environmental emblem of the ECPU, the Doctor, wearing an ill-fitting diving-suit, was awaiting the signal for him to drop into the murky waters of the River Thames.

'Please be careful, Doctor.' As she helped Mike and Helen to adjust the helmet on the Doctor's diving suit, Sarah Jane had to shout to be heard.

The Doctor's reply was muffled, and only barely audible. 'Just make sure you keep a hold on my lifeline!'

'And remember,' called Mike, 'You've got enough oxygen for just one hour. And make sure you keep clear of the sandbanks. They're impossible to walk on.'

The Doctor gave a thumb-up sign to show that he understood. Then he sat down on the edge of the boat, with the sea behind him. To Sarah Jane, the next moment or so seemed like an eternity. But finally, one of the motor-launch crew gave the signal, and with a loud splash the Doctor threw himself backwards into the muddy Estuary.

Sarah Jane, Mike, Helen, and the crew watched him disappear in a whirlpool of bubbles. As a ship's horn sounded in the far distance, none of them were sure whether they would ever see the Doctor again.

2

INTO THE DEPTHS

Although the air temperature during the afternoon was still very high, the murky waters of the Thames Estuary were cold and unfriendly. The Doctor's dark and eerie shape floated majestically towards the seabed, and as it did so it left behind a long trail of tiny bubbles which immediately struggled back to the surface.

The Doctor, who was not a good swimmer at the best of times, found the whole experience quite awesome. He was in a lonesome world, where human life seemed to have no place, and was in fact an intrusion. And yet, in some ways, it was all quite beautiful. Unlike the shoals of tiny fish that swam past him, he found his own slow-motion movements reminiscent to walking in space; nothing could be achieved in haste. But it could not be denied that the waters of the Estuary were dirty. On the way down from the surface he had seen only too much evidence of man's contempt for nature, with litter of all description dumped into the sea or river to pollute the water and destroy its marine life. It was a very depressing sight.

When the Doctor finally reached the bed of the Estuary, his rubber boots sent up a cloud of sand which almost completely obscured his view. But gradually he broke clear, and slowly made his way in a westerly direction towards the open sea. On his way he passed all sorts of debris from old boats and dinghies that had either foundered in bad weather, or fallen victim to enemy action during the first two world wars of the twentieth century. At times, the Doctor felt as though he were in some vast underwater graveyard, and at any moment expected to see the ghosts of mariners floating unnervingly across his path. Just for good measure, he checked his umbilical lifeline cord to ensure that he could make a quick escape if he needed to.

'Doctor! Are you all right?' Sarah Jane's anxious voice echoed tinnily through the Doctor's underwater walkie-talkie. 'Where are you? Over.'

The Doctor wiped his visor and called back through the built-in microphone attached to the inside of the helmet. 'I'm just approaching the wreck of an old freight barge or something. At least that's what it looks like. Visibility's not good down here. Over.'

'Any sign of the meteor? Over.'

'Not so far. I'll keep you posted. Over.'

The voice at the surface suddenly changed. 'Doctor, can you hear me? This is Mike Ridgewell. Over.'

'I hear you, Mike. Over.'

Mike's voice was tense, and he was speaking louder than he needed to. 'Listen to me now. We're keeping your lifeline as taut as we can. If we lose radio contact, tug it as hard as you can. Over and out.'

Inside his diving helmet, the Doctor grinned. 'Don't worry – I will. Over and out.' As he continued on his way, a vast shoal of herring fluttered towards him, then at the last moment suddenly darted off to his right, to disappear into the wreck of the old barge. There were plenty of other fish around, some big with bulging eyes, some small, and as he moved cautiously on the soft Estuary bed, small crabs scattered in all directions. The Doctor watched them all with a feeling of deep foreboding.

Fortunately, his diving-suit was heavily protected against

14

the radioactivity that was now contaminating the sea water. The fish, darting in and around him, would soon discover that they were not so lucky.

Once he was well clear of the old sunken barge, the Doctor made his way slowly and precariously towards a bleak stretch of seabed, which, for one moment, gave him the impression that he was walking on the surface of the moon. However, after ten minutes or so, he gradually became aware that not only was the sandy bed of the Estuary clear of debris, but that the water itself seemed to be completely without any sign of marine life. It was a strange feeling, and the Doctor started to feel uneasy.

A few minutes later, he approached what seemed to be an underwater sandbank. But it was only when he drew nearer that he realized how the sandbank had been formed, for immediately in front of him was what looked like the mouth of some vast underwater cavern. There was now no doubt in the Doctor's mind that he had found what he was looking for; the build-up of sand had clearly been caused by the impact of the falling meteorite. Checking his wristwatch, the Doctor realized that he had already used up half his oxygen, leaving him with no more than thirty minutes to explore any further. However, he decided that he had to go on, so, after carefully peering inside the cavern, he floated through the opening and finally landed clumsily on all fours.

'What's going on down there?' The sudden tug on the Doctor's lifeline cord had caused Mike to panic at the surface. 'Are you all right, Doctor? Is anything wrong? Over.'

The Doctor picked himself up, and started to unravel the lifeline cord from around his legs. 'I'm perfectly all right,' he called, determined not to give any clue to his undignified landing. 'Just taking a good look round, that's all. Over.'

'Do hurry, Doctor!' This time it was Sarah Jane's anxious call again. 'You've only got twenty-six more minutes. Over and out.' As she spoke, her voice started to break up with persistent static until it finally cut out altogether.

The Doctor decided to wait no longer. As he moved off into the darkness of the cavern, he found it necessary to use the special high-powered torch he had clipped onto the front of his diving-suit. When he turned it on, the ray pierced the darkness immediately, illuminating the walls of a huge tunnel of sand and rock, the floor of which sloped down gradually to an even greater depth. Moving with absolute caution, he directed the rays of the torch to the strange symmetrical marks that were embedded into the tunnel walls. Somehow, the Doctor found them only too familiar, and it took him no time at all to realize that this was no man-made tunnel. The marks had been torn into the walls by the claws of some enormous sea creature.

Half walking, half floating, his umbilical lifeline cord closely following on behind, the Doctor proceeded along the tunnel with absolute caution. Within a moment or so, he found himself drawn towards a vast source of fluorescent light, so bright that he immediately turned off his torch and replaced it in his belt. The fluorescent light seemed to be faintly green in colour, and was pulsating. As he drew closer to the light, it was positively dazzling, and he had to shield his eyes with one hand. Finally, he came to a stop, when he suddenly realized that he had reached the heart of the huge cavern, which seemed almost the size of some vast indoor stadium. Quickly activating the glare reflector inside his helmet, the Doctor was able to see through the dazzling light which was completely flooding the Cavern. What he saw, however, was exactly what he had expected. The light was coming from a huge, cylindrically-shaped spacecraft, the remains of its metallic frame glistening in an overwhelming pool of blinding fluorescence. The structure of the spacecraft looked as though it was made of a metal which the Doctor was not familiar with, but what he did notice was that the surface was heavily scorched, probably by friction on its entry into Earth's atmosphere.

A few minutes later, the Doctor found his way into the alien spacecraft through the huge access door which had been left wide open. Once inside, he was astonished at the vast array of technology that had been used to build the machine. But the control panels and switches were unlike anything he had ever seen before, and were clearly meant to be operated by some kind of ingenious remote control. He was particularly intrigued to see that most of the wall space was covered by hundreds of small, rectangular video screens all bevelled at sharp angles. However, apart from the blinding emerald glare emanating from the exterior surface of the machine, everything inside the spacecraft was, to all intents and purposes, absolutely dead.

By now, the Doctor realized that he was letting his curiosity get the better of him, for his watch showed that he now only had ten more minutes of oxygen time left. But as he turned to leave by the way he had come in, the sea water around him suddenly picked up a humming sound, which came and went, swirling in and out of his every movement. And then the sound was picked up by a vibration which quite literally rocked the spacecraft, as though it was being affected by earth tremors. The Doctor's only thoughts now were to get out of the monstrous machine as fast as he could, but it was no easy task, for his lifeline was caught up on some of the access door mechanism. It took him several minutes to free himself, and by the time he eventually did, a red light suddenly appeared on his oxygen supply indicator showing: '*DANGER! FIVE MINUTES.*'

The spacecraft was trembling violently as if in an earthquake when the Doctor finally managed to leap out of the machine and float back onto the sand floor below. But the leap was a clumsy one, which left him sprawled out flat on his back. With the seconds ticking away, his only aim now was to get back down the tunnel and be pulled to the surface of the Estuary as soon as possible. But, just as he was about to recover his balance, he was suddenly chilled to find something touching his shoulder from behind. He turned with a start, and was horrified to find himself face to face with the hollowed eyes of a skull. In great panic, he managed to stand up and start pushing himself away, but as he went more human skeleton heads, arms, and legs, were floating all around him; it was like being in an underwater graveyard. The Doctor had no time to consider who or what the skeletons were or where

17

they came from. His main task was to reach the tunnel and get back to the surface as fast as he possibly could.

With just two or three minutes to go before his oxygen was exhausted, the Doctor used all his strength to push against the underwater pressure. But in his haste to reach the tunnel again, he had kicked up a cloud of watery sand, which was obscuring his vision and making his progress hazardous. It was only when the sand cloud finally cleared that he found his return to the surface was going to be no easy matter. Suddenly, the vast underwater cavern was echoing to the rumbling sound of the huge half-human, half-fish creature. And as it swam out from the tunnel, the creature's eyes pierced through the fluorescence in the cavern like two shimmering emerald rays of light.

'Doctor to Base! Doctor to Base!' The Doctor's voice was desperate as he tried to make contact with Mike and Sarah Jane at the surface. But all he could get from his radio transmitter was loud static and no response from any of the ECPU team.

As the creature landed on its webbed feet and lurched almost in slow motion towards the Doctor, each of its silvery scales were like reflectors, shooting particles of light in every direction. And then its mouth opened to reveal sharp, pointed teeth, and it roared, sending deafening sound waves through the dense, cloudy water. All around the cavern, the disjointed skeleton bones scattered in every direction.

'*ONE MINUTE*'. The red light in the Doctor's oxygen supply unit was flashing on danger level. In a last desperate act, he tugged with all his might at his lifeline.

As the Doctor slowly backed away towards the tunnel exit, the creature reached out, its talons glistening in the emerald light.

The Doctor struggled desperately to keep clear of the creature's advance, until suddenly: '*EMPTY*'. The red light in the Doctor's oxygen supply unit flashed just once, then disappeared. Almost immediately the Doctor's helmet was airless, and the visor started to steam over. He could see absolutely nothing. But as the creature reached out to grab

18

at him, the Doctor suddenly found himself being tugged hard from behind by his lifeline. Within seconds he was back in the tunnel, and then in the higher Estuary waters.

Struggling for breath, the Doctor's body had no more life in it to reach the surface unaided. Up, up he went. But all was darkness. He could see or feel nothing, absolutely nothing...

'It's a miracle! An absolute miracle!' Mike Ridgewell could hardly believe his eyes, for the Doctor was actually sitting up in bed in the First Aid Unit at ECPU, eyes open, eating a hearty meal of scrambled eggs on toast. 'By the time we pulled you out of the water, you must have been without oxygen for over five minutes. It's impossible for any ordinary human being to survive after that.'

Sarah Jane smiled to herself. Since when, she thought, had the Doctor been an 'ordinary human being'?

'I can assure you, Mike,' said the Doctor, crunching the last piece of toast and wiping his fingers on the bedsheet, 'my oxygen supply was the least of my problems. I'd much rather lose my breath than be stripped alive by the vicious teeth of a Pescaton.'

This was the first time Sarah Jane, Mike, or Helen had heard such a name, and they all exchanged puzzled looks. 'Pescaton?' asked Helen warily. 'What's that?'

'Cunning, ravenous sea-creatures.' The Doctor's expression was deadly serious as he spoke. 'They're half human, half fish, and they have the most voracious appetite, I can tell you.'

Helen peered over the top of her spectacles. She was very suspicious of the Doctor's story. 'Fish that are half human? I've never heard that one before.'

Sarah Jane turned on her immediately. 'Well, you would have done, if you'd been with us down on that beach last night.'

The Doctor was already getting out of bed and putting on his trousers over his long-leg underpants. 'They're aggressive brutes.' And without looking at the others he added

19

pointedly, 'Carnivorous too, unfortunately. Their origins are in the *carchariidae*.'

This time Sarah Jane looked absolutely baffled. 'Say that again?'

'The shark species.' It was Mike who answered, but it was the Doctor he was watching as he spoke.

'The shark species!' Helen took off her spectacles in disbelief. 'Are you saying there's a man-eating shark out there in the Thames Estuary?'

The Doctor looked up only briefly from putting on his shoes. 'Something like that.'

Mike was now in the depths of depression. He waited for the Doctor to finish tying his shoelaces, then asked directly, 'Doctor. Did you see anything of our – of our CPU team?'

The Doctor had been waiting for this question, and tried to avoid the question by taking a very long time to tie up his last shoelace.

'Please, Doctor,' insisted Mike. 'I have to know.'

Reluctantly, the Doctor looked up, and looked Mike straight in the eyes. 'Yes. I did see them.'

That was all Mike needed to know, and he asked no more questions. Some of the CPU team who went down to search for the meteorite were personal friends of Mike's and their loss had caused him great distress.

'I really don't understand any of this,' Helen said, suddenly. 'I thought we were supposed to be looking for a meteorite, not a man-eating shark.'

The Doctor immediately became very succinct and practical. 'Neither a meteor nor a man-eating shark, Miss Briggs. What you have down there on the seabed is an enormous Pescaton spacecraft.'

'A spacecraft?' Mike, who had gone to look out of the window, turned back with a start.

'Fish who can build spacecraft?' Sarah Jane asked sceptically. 'Who can fly off to other planets?'

The Doctor was now putting on his coat. 'Yes, I know it sounds fantastic, Sarah Jane. But the Pescaton civilization has developed a technology which is far superior to anything on Earth. These creatures possess — unnatural powers. They're able to anticipate our every move.'

'You're not asking us to believe all this, are you?' said Helen, clumsily. 'Fish with a high IQ.' She started to laugh. 'The tabloids will have a field-day with this one! Come on now, Doctor. You *can't* be serious?'

The Doctor waited for her to stop answering before he replied. He didn't like to be ridiculed by someone to whom he had taken an instant dislike. 'I can assure you, Miss Briggs, I am most serious.'

Mike could sense the Doctor's growing irritation with Helen, so he came across to him and asked quietly. 'Where do these "creatures" come from, Doctor?'

'From the planet Pesca. It's in the outer galaxies.'

'Pesca?' Mike was puzzled. At school, one of his favourite subjects was astronomy, but he couldn't remember ever hearing of such a planet.

'Once, it was rich with vast oceans, and forests as green and lush as anything you would find on Earth. But they made mistakes. They misused their natural resources and became greedy for power. They fought amongst themselves, until their planet was reduced to nothing more than a desert, a vast wilderness. It was hell to set foot on the place.'

'So you've actually been to this planet?' asked Sarah Jane. 'What d'you call it — Pesca?'

'Well, of course I've been to Pesca. I know the place well. The last time I was there was late fifteenth century. Back in the good old days.'

Sarah Jane threw him a sceptical glance. 'Fifteenth century! Just how old are you, Doctor, anyway?'

The Doctor grinned back at her. 'Trade secret.' But then he was suddenly aware that Mike and Helen were listening to his exchange with Sarah Jane in total astonishment. So he quickly gave them a reassuring smile. 'Only in my research of course.'

As the Doctor put on his hat and made for the door, Mike quickly followed him and Sarah Jane into the outer office. 'Doctor!' he called.

The Doctor stopped at the front door, and turned.

Mike came to him, and lowered his voice so that the secretary at her desk could not overhear them. 'Doctor, I don't know who you are, or where you come from. But if what you say is true – if there really is some kind of an alien spacecraft on the seabed out there – what effect is it going to have on our environment?'

The Doctor pursed his lips for a moment, then wiped them with the back of his hand. 'Mike. Pesca is a dying planet – it has been dying for thousands of years. By now, every ocean will be steaming with evaporation because the sun is drawing closer all the time.'

It was now obvious that Mike, unlike Helen, was taking the Doctor really seriously. 'If it is possible,' he asked, 'if it is possible that there is some kind of alien creature roaming around out there in the Estuary, then what is it doing here? Why has it chosen to come to this planet?'

The Doctor moved to the front door and opened it. Mike and Sarah Jane joined him there, and paused to take in the fresh sea air of a summer's evening. 'The Pescaton population is desperate to escape from their planet before it completely disintegrates,' said the Doctor, with utmost urgency. Then, turning to Mike, he continued, 'This is what they want. This is what they need. Planet Earth! If they are to survive as a race, as a species, they must escape from the catastrophe of their own making.'

Sarah Jane now looked very scared. 'That creature – the one we saw on the beach – you're saying it found its way here to Earth, across millions of miles of space?'

'An advance guard, Sarah Jane.' The Doctor turned to look at her. It was a look that she had always dreaded. 'That creature is the first of the Pescaton migration.'

As all three turned to look out at the sea, the Estuary had turned a deep crimson colour, with the sun, like a huge ball of fire, just dipping into the far horizon.

And beyond the Estuary was the mighty River Thames, stretching for as far as the eye could see, right into the very heart of London.

3

PANIC!

Young Jess and Tommy had both been living out rough for over a year. They usually bunked down in a shop front in the Strand, just off Trafalgar Square in London, but in the summer months they prefered to take their sleeping bags down to their favourite spot on an elevated stone walkway alongside the River Thames near the Tower of London. Here, they were not only shielded from the wind, but could also light a small fire without attracting too much attention from the Police River launches which patrolled the river every hour or so. Jess came from Newcastle-on-Tyne, in the North of England. He left home after a violent quarrel with his father, who didn't seem to understand that a boy of seventeen is no longer a kid, but someone who should be allowed to make his own decisions about how he wants to live. Tommy ran away from his home in Surrey, not because he didn't get on with his aunt and uncle who brought him up, but because he'd heard what a great time teenage kids like himself could have if they moved into the big city. Both were to be sadly disillusioned, for ever since they teamed up a year before, they had become virtual beggars, relying on any coins or bits and pieces of food people in the street could give them. Some people called them 'drop-outs', and sneered at them as they passed by. Others thought that all they needed was someone who would be willing to spare the time to stop and talk to them, and listen to their problems.

Their nightly companion on the Thames embankment was old Ben, who had lived out rough for years. But his reasons for 'dropping-out' were very different from those of his young friends. For the first part of his life, Ben had held a good job in a City bank, where he earned a decent salary which enabled him to buy most of the things he wanted and to enjoy the company of his steady girlfriend. But after more than ten years of this, the pulverizing routine had driven him spare, and he had to get away from it all. Ever since then he had been cut off from society as he knew it, and the only roof he had known was the sky above.

'Yer won't get much out of there ternight,' murmured old Ben as he watched young Tommy trying to fish in the river, using only a piece of string with a bent pin on the end. Ben himself was much more occupied with finishing off the remains of a small tin of baked beans, which he had heated over the dying embers of the fire. 'Yer don't get much fish when the tide's out.'

Tommy wiped his nose on the back of his hand, and held onto the fishing line with his other hand. 'We got sumfink the uvver night,' he said. 'The tide was much lower then.'

'Please yerself,' sneered Ben, scraping inside the empty baked beans tin with his finger. 'But yer're wastin' yer time.'

'Why don't you two go ter sleep,' complained Jess, who still spoke in a strong Newcastle accent. He was tucked up in his sleeping bag, using a pile of old newspapers for a pillow. 'What's the point er fishin' in the middle of the night?'

Tommy didn't reply. He was determined to persevere, mainly because he was hungry. The river was full of fish, that he knew. And a lot more besides, for he had often pulled out old tin cans, discarded rugs and carpets, and any amount of take-away wrappers. People didn't care what they dumped in the river, as long as they got rid of it quickly and without trouble.

Old Ben licked his fingers and started his great ritual of

settling down for the night, or what was left of it. He didn't possess the luxury of a sleeping bag, but he had accumulated a good pile of old newspapers and cardboard boxes, which were perfectly adequate protection against the night air, at least in summer. Within a few minutes, he was snoring loudly.

Tommy decided to try his luck closer to the water's edge, so he moved down onto the narrow stretch of shingled beach. The water itself was quite calm, with hardly a ripple on the surface. There was no breeze, and the night was quite humid, although because of the heavy clouds, it was very dark. However, above him in the distance, the headlights of a solitary car were seen darting across the majestic Tower Bridge, which itself was illuminated by floodlights throwing a magnificent reflection on the surface of the river which it spanned.

To Tommy's surprise, he had only been fishing for a few minutes when his primitive line suddenly tugged at his hand. With great excitement, he started to pull in. But the string refused to budge, and appeared to be caught on something. Without any care for his worn-out trainers and torn jeans, Tommy quickly waded into the water right up to his knees, tugging his pathetic piece of fishing string as hard as he dared. But still it would not budge. This was going to be quite a battle, he thought, for already there was a shimmer on the surface of the water.

Back on the elevated stone platform, it was Jess who first noticed the slight vibration. His eyes suddenly sprang open, he sat up with a start, and he immediately looked around. 'Tommy!' he yelled. 'Where are yer? What yer up to?'

Old Ben stopped snoring for a moment, but only turned on to one side, still fast asleep.

Jess couldn't see anything in the dark, but he sensed something. He felt uneasy. 'Tommy?' he called again in a low, strangulated whisper. 'Git yersel back 'ere!' He had only begun to panic when he suddenly heard a distant weird hissing sound, followed by the furious splashing of water.

'Tommy!' This time he yelled louder.

Old Ben merely grunted in his sleep. He clearly thought he was having a nightmare.

Jess unzipped his sleeping bag, stood up, and tried to peer into the darkness. Nothing. Cautiously, he decided to go down to look for Tommy on the beach. As he jumped down onto the shingle, the sound of his own footsteps made him even more nervous. 'Tommy!' His voice sounded thin and nervous. 'Come on now. Stop muckin' around! What yer up to?' It was at that precise moment that he got his first smell of fish. In all the time he had been sleeping alongside the river, he had never noticed it before. But it was strong, like being out at sea in a fishing-boat. Perhaps Tommy had been lucky after all, he thought.

'What yer got, Tommy?' he called warily. 'Got somethin', 'ave yer?' As he spoke, there was a tremendous commotion in the water beside him, and as he turned to look out at the river, his blood was chilled to see the shape of an enormous creature emerging from the water, its penetrating emerald eyes illuminating everything in their path. Jess had no time to yell for help. In what seemed like a fraction of a second, the monstrous apparition had overwhelmed him, and dragged him back into the depths of the river.

At first, old Ben thought his nightmare had woken him. But it hadn't. It was the rumbling sound. Sitting up with a start, his eyes immediately shot towards the river's edge. His blood was immediately chilled by the devastating things he could see through the bright green glare, which was reflected in his own transfixed eyes.

Making quite sure that both Jess and Tommy were not around, Ben quickly rolled up their sleeping bags, tucked them firmly under his arms, and after collecting his own few things together, he hurried off back to the embankment as fast as his old legs would carry him.

The Doctor's old friend, the astronomer Professor Bud Emmerson, hadn't changed a bit since they last met during one of the Doctor's previous generations. True, he was a little older, now in his mid-sixties, but he was just as fat as he always had been, which seemed to put his tall, massive body out of proportion with his head, which was really quite small. And his hair was now almost white, which was easily detectable despite the fact that he had cropped it short. A few years previously, Bud had been a well-known comedy actor in British films and television, but he had finally decided to abandon his career in favour of his first love, astronomy. And with the help of the Royal Astronomical Society, he had built the now legendary North London observatory, which settled quite naturally on the peak of Highgate Hill, with the whole of London's skyline spread out before it.

'Bit of a tall order that, you know, Doctor.' Emmerson spoke with his usual fast, boyish enthusiasm. 'Fish from outer space, you say? Well, at least it's original, I suppose. Probably make a good film, I suspect.'

'I'm serious, Bud,' warned the Doctor, grim-faced. He and Sarah Jane had been at the Observatory for over an hour, and only now had they been able to get the Professor to listen to the urgent reason which had brought them there. 'I can assure you there is very intense activity on Pesca.'

'I know that, dear boy,' replied the Professor with a twinkle in his eye. 'I sent a report to the Royal Society about it months ago. Don't worry, the old girl's been keeping a close watch on Pesca.' He smiled up gratefully at his giant F2 Telescope, which was pointing straight up through the domed roof towards the sky, and gave the eyepiece an affectionate pat. Indeed, one of the reasons the Doctor and his old friend had come together in the first place had been when the Professor had first pinpointed the planet Pesca in the night sky.

'Bud,' pressed the Doctor urgently. 'I know you've never accepted the possibility that there could be any form of life on Pesca, but you've got to believe me when I tell you that there is.' As he spoke, his voice boomed out an echo around the dome. 'These creatures have found a way to escape from their own dying environment. They've developed a space vehicle that can take them to any planet which has an atmosphere they can survive in.'

The Professor peered casually through the eyepiece of his

beloved telescope. 'If such a life form exists, I'm not surprised they want to get away from their own planet. There's hardly any ozone protection left around Pesca. It's only a matter of time before the sun blows the place to smithereens!' Reluctantly, he left the telescope, and climbed down the three metal steps from the observation platform, to join the Doctor and Sarah Jane in the main hall. 'So what d'you think these Pescaton things are looking for on our planet?'

The Doctor did not hesitate in his reply. 'The sea. Salt water.'

The Professor frowned sceptically. 'You think they could survive in Earth's oceans?'

'I don't know. But the one we've seen is having a damned good try.'

Sarah Jane interrupted immediately. 'The creature is really horrible, Professor. You should see it for yourself. It's so aggressive, so . . . ugly. I've never been so scared in all my life.' She went on to describe the Pescaton, and how it had covered the TARDIS in a thick mass of a green sticky substance.

The Professor smiled momentarily. 'These creatures sound a bit like one or two television directors I know,' he chuckled.

'This is no joke, Bud,' insisted the Doctor sternly. 'I know the Pescatons well. They're a mean, ruthless civilization. They've destroyed their own planet, and if we allow them to get a foothold here, they'll destroy our planet too.'

The Professor took his pipe from his pocket. 'We don't have to wait for the Pescatons to do that,' he said, putting his pipe into his mouth without lighting it. 'We're already making a very good job of that ourselves.' The Doctor and Sarah Jane followed him across the hall, as he made his way to the long, rectangular observation window which overlooked the vast panorama of London's skyline. 'How can I help?' he asked suddenly.

'Alert every astronomer you can. If there are reports of meteorites falling to Earth anywhere, we have to know.'

The Professor tapped his teeth with his unlit pipe. 'You think they could be Pescaton space vehicles?'

28

'It's possible. But we have to make sure.'

'And what happens if they are Pescaton creatures?' He turned to look at the Doctor, whom he trusted well enough to take seriously. 'How will you deal with them?'

The Doctor looked the Professor straight in the eye. There was a note of desperation in his voice. 'I haven't the faintest idea,' he said quietly.

Sarah Jane looked at both men. Here she was, she thought, only ten years or so from the period in time she left behind, with the chance to write up one of the greatest scoops in history. And yet, somehow, the whole idea of it terrified her.

Back at the ECPU Base at Shoeburyness, Mike Ridgewell and his team were dealing with dozens of calls about the pollution of beaches by an unidentified sticky green substance. Forensic analysis of the substance had shown that it contained a small element of radioactivity, so Mike had warned the local town council to declare the contaminated areas prohibited. What was even more worrying was that local fishing trawlers were coming back with empty nets, and one trawler skipper had reported that the previous evening he and his crew had caught sight of a very large fish indeed, swimming just below the surface of the water, and heading off down the river towards London. The skipper said that although they were unable to identify the kind of fish they saw, it was certainly bigger than a whale.

Some time later, Mike, Helen, and the ECPU team, all wearing protective anti-contamination suits, were down on the beach checking out the path of the sticky green substance. But their greatest shock was to find the small beach huts all covered in a hardened shroud of the substance, into which were embedded shingles, dead fish, minute crustaceans, and thousands of tiny empty seashells. It was as though some giant spider had cast a web over its prey.

'This is absurd!' said Helen, suddenly ripping off her protective helmet. 'Anyone with even a bit of intelligence can see that this isn't anything to do with creatures from outer space. There's some kind of animal on the loose. Has anyone checked the local zoos?'

Mike removed his helmet, and took a deep breath of sea air. 'Have you ever seen an animal that can do that?' He nodded towards the beach-hut shrouds.

'Come off it now, Mike. This is not science fiction, this is reality! You're not going to tell me that you actually believe this Doctor person – whatever he is?'

Mike stared out towards the Estuary, a grim expression on his face. 'I don't know who or what to believe, Helen. All I know is that I've lost two of my best friends out there. Something's going on that we just don't understand.' He turned back to her. 'Just remember,' he said. 'The Doctor's the only one that's actually seen where that meteorite fell.'

'Precisely! But we know nothing at all about this man, who he is, or where he comes from? How d'you know we can trust him?'

'I don't. But I can't see what possible motive he could have for making up such a story.'

'And neither do I. That's what I don't like about it.'

'What do you mean?'

Helen took out a cigarette, and quickly lit it. 'I just don't like the man, that's all. I don't believe in all this eccentric bit. And as for that girl – who is she? His daughter?'

Mike sighed, and started to move off along the beach.

Helen followed him, puffing out smoke from her cigarette as she went. 'Look, Mike. I'm not trying to be difficult, but everyone knows it was a meteorite that came down that night, not a stupid spacecraft.'

'We don't know that, Helen!' Mike was getting irritated with her. 'Apart from the Doctor, no living person has actually seen what it is that's sitting on the seabed out there.'

'My point precisely,' said Helen, her dyed blonde curls blowing in the breeze. 'But there's one way of finding out.'

'I'm not sending anyone else down into that water.'

Finding it difficult to catch up, Helen called after him. 'You don't have to. I'll go myself.'

Mike stopped with a start. Then, realizing the implication of Helen's remark, he turned quickly, and pointing a warning

30

finger at her, said, 'No, Helen! And that's an order!'

Helen merely smiled back at him, drew on her cigarette, and flicked it into the sea.

'Mike!'

Mike turned immediately, to find Pete, one of the younger men from his team, calling to him from the beach-hut shrouds nearby.

'Over here – quick!'

Mike hurried across to his team, leaving Helen to make her way back to the Unit Base.

'There's someone inside,' said Pete excitedly. 'We can hear him calling.'

'What!' Utterly shocked, Mike threw his protection helmet onto the shingled beach, and moved closer to the shroud of one of the beach huts. 'How d'you know?'

'He's been calling. Sound's like a feller. If you put your ear close, you can just hear him.'

Mike pressed as close as he could to the hardened substance of the shroud and called out, 'Is anyone there?'

For a moment, there was absolute silence.

'Is anyone there?' Mike called out, louder this time. 'Can you hear me?'

Suddenly, the distant voice of what sounded like a teenage boy was heard, yelling out as loud as he could. 'I can hear you! Get me out of here! I can hardly breathe!'

'Don't panic!' shouted Mike at the top of his voice. 'We'll get to you as soon as we can.'

Within a few moments, every member of the team was hammering at the hardened substance of the shroud with anything they could lay their hands on. But the Pescaton creature had done its work well and the substance it had used for its weblike shroud was harder than the thickest concrete. Half an hour later, a heavy pneumatic drill was brought in to attack the deadly wall of hardened slime.

No one could be sure how soon it would be before the creature returned to claim its prey.

From now on it was a race against time.

4

A PREMONITION

The Doctor and Sarah Jane made their way on foot along the Victoria Embankment. It was late afternoon, and the city streets were crowded with traffic, tourists, and people making their way to and from double-decker buses and underground stations. On the opposite side of the river, the white concrete buildings of the great arts complex of the South Bank were bathed in red by a rather watery sun which had managed to break only intermittently through the grey clouds.

It was over half an hour since the Doctor last spoke to Sarah Jane, for he was deep in thought, hands clasped behind his back, eyes glued to the surface of the river with its usual array of sightseeing boats, freight barges, and the occasional police river launch. He didn't quite know what he was looking for. All he knew was that he had an uncomfortable feeling about the scene before him. Something was telling him to shout out to the people of London and warn them to be prepared for something. After all, it would not be the first time Britain's capital city had faced up to impending disaster. And it would certainly not be the last.

Eventually, Sarah Jane could remain silent no longer. 'Is it possible the Pescaton could have reached as far as this,

Doctor?'

The Doctor came out of his near trance, and frowned. 'I don't know, Sarah Jane. But my guess is that if it has, the people of London are in for a nasty shock.'

'But you are convinced that there's only one of them?'

'As far as I can tell.' The Doctor took off his hat for a moment, and fanned himself in the humid afternoon air. 'Of course, they need plenty of room to land their spacecraft. That's obviously why they've used the Estuary. But the Pescatons are unpredictable creatures. You never know what they're going to get up to.'

As they walked on, a pleasure boat was just passing under Waterloo Bridge. It was full of cheering schoolchildren, and camera-clicking foreign tourists.

About an hour later, they were a short distance from the tourists' favourite London attraction, the Tower of London, with its heavy grey walls and turrets cutting a dramatic shape against the early summer evening sky. And just beyond that, the two sections of Tower Bridge were just closing after allowing a tall-masted sailing boat to pass beneath.

It was at this moment that the Doctor first noticed some rather unusual activity which was taking place down by the river's edge. The tide was out, a police launch was hovering in midstream, and a cluster of police cars was gathered on the road nearby. The narrow shingled beach was bristling with black uniforms, and bobbing in and out of the water was a police diving team who were clearly searching the riverbed.

Sarah Jane quickly followed the Doctor down to the police barrier which had been erected on the stone platform and steps leading down to the beach. A small crowd of onlookers had gathered there, but were kept back by two burly bobbies who looked as though they would take no nonsense from anyone.

'That's as far as you go, sir – thank you.' The elder of the two bobbies, with a thick black beard, was courteous, but determined not to let the Doctor pass the barrier.

'What's going on?' asked the Doctor with mounting

curiosity.

'Nothing that concerns you, sir. Now keep well back, please.'

At this point, Sarah Jane stepped forward, holding up a small plastic identity card with her photograph on it. 'Press!' she said curtly, practically pushing the card under the policeman's nose. 'Let me pass, please.'

He took no more than a passing glance at the card, and raised the barrier for Sarah Jane to pass. But as she went she called back casually, 'He's with me.'

The Doctor was absolutely astonished by Sarah Jane's cool initiative. If the policeman had taken the trouble to look more carefully at the date of the press card, he would have noticed that it was about ten years before its time! He hurriedly followed Sarah Jane, smiling profusely and raising his hat to the scowling policeman as he passed.

The first thing the Doctor noticed on his way down to the beach, were the remains of a small bonfire on the elevated stone platform alongside the river. The beach itself was absolutely crawling with policemen, divers, men and women in white jackets, and a photographer, who was taking flashlight pictures of practically everything around. The Doctor immediately made contact with the Police Inspector in charge of the incident, explaining that he was an official from the Department of the Environment.

'There was some kind of a rumpus down here last night,' said the Inspector, who was watching carefully everything that was going on around him. 'We got a tip-off from a woman who was walking her dog along the road up there. Apparently, there were three people kipping rough down here – one old boy and two young 'uns. We know who they are. We've seen 'em down here ourselves most nights. Anyway, when this woman came back later with her dog, she heard a hell of a rumpus going on. Couldn't see much, but she heard a lot of splashing about in the water. After that, she didn't see the two young 'uns any more. But she did see the old boy make off as fast as he could. Seems he took the young 'uns' things with him.'

'How very curious,' said the Doctor, trying to sound as naïve as possible.

'That's not the only thing that's curious.' The Inspector was looking out towards the river. 'What I don't understand is this vibration the woman talked about.'

'Vibration?' asked Sarah Jane, in her best inquisitive reporter voice. 'What kind of vibration?'

The Inspector aimlessly scratched the stubble on his chin. 'Hard to tell really. She said there was this rumbling sound, then the whole riverside started to shake. When she looked down at the beach again, the two young 'uns had gone, and the river itself was covered in a green light.'

The Doctor tensed, and Sarah Jane felt her blood turn to ice.

'Anyway,' continued the Inspector, 'we're digging around the river bed to see what we can find. Nothing so far though.'

Sarah Jane swallowed hard, and tried to summon up enough courage to continue her questioning. 'Who were these people? Have you any idea?'

'Oh yes, we know' em all right. The two young 'uns were a couple of runaways. We've had 'em inside a couple of times, just to warm 'em up a bit with a cup of cocoa. The old boy's been knocking around the streets for years. His name's Ben. Crafty old −. If you fell asleep for even five minutes he'd rob you of your false teeth − if you had any!' The Inspector self-consciously tapped his own teeth with one finger, as if to prove that they were not false.

The Doctor was already moving off on his own along the beach. As he went he found all the signs he was looking for: the same kind of disturbance in the shingles that he had seen back on the Essex coastal beach, and the same traces of green, slimy substance.

'It's the Pescaton, isn't it, Doctor?' Sarah Jane had rejoined him, taking in the whole bizarre scence that was being played out on the beach as she approached. 'The Pescaton has found its way upriver from the Estuary.'

The Doctor was crouched down on the beach, inspecting the green slime. 'I don't think there's any doubt about it,

Sarah Jane. These creatures can move faster in the water than any fish half their size.'

'But why does it have to attack everything in sight for absolutely no reason at all?' Sarah Jane crouched alongside him, and lowered her voice. 'What does the Pescaton want, Doctor? What does this dreadful creature want?'

The Doctor looked out towards the river where two divers were just leaping off the police launch to continue their search of the riverbed. 'I don't know, Sarah Jane. But there's someone wandering the streets who might be able to tell us.'

Old Ben had carefully hidden the two sleeping bags and the other meagre possessions he had stolen from Jess and Tommy. He had concealed them in his usual hiding place, an old unused dustbin behind a cafe where he sometimes cadged for titbits of food. Since his two young friends had disappeared into the river the night before, he had tried to keep a low profile on the West End streets that were his daily haunt. Most days he would find some shopfront to squat down in front of, with a piece of cardboard around his neck with the words 'OUT OF WORK. OLD AND HUNGRY' scrawled roughly across it. But today he kept away from public places, because for some reason he couldn't understand, he was feeling guilty. After all, he thought, whatever happened to the young 'uns was no fault of his, and as they wouldn't be needing their sleeping bags any more, he saw no reason why he shouldn't have them.

By the time evening came, Ben thought it would be safe for him to venture out from his daytime resting place in St James's Park. So after splashing a little water on his face in the lake there, he made his way down Piccadilly and into Leicester Square, where for a moment or two he watched the buskers singing and dancing and making more money in five minutes than he made in a whole day.

A little later he was in the Chinese district behind Leicester Square, where he immediately made his way to his regular haunt, Chung-Li's restaurant, where the owner was very sympathetic to him, and always invited him into the kitchen to finish up any pork spare ribs left over from the customers' plates. He shuffled into the back yard, approached the kitchen door, tapped on it, and entered.

'Evening all!' he called. 'What's on the menu ternight then?'

The cook and his assistant were waiting for the old cadger, but for once, were not grinning broadly at him. In a moment he was to discover why.

'Evening, Ben.'

Ben turned with a start. Two uniformed officers were waiting for him. He knew them well. They knew him too.

By floodlight, Mike Ridgewell and his team, using a powerful pneumatic drill, were finally managing to break off pieces of the hardened slime shroud which was covering the beach hut and the prisoner trapped inside. It had taken hours of hard work to get this far, for the solid slime was tougher than any concrete or building mix the men had ever come across. But they persevered, hoping that if they could make a hole through the shroud, then at least the teenage boy trapped inside would be able to breathe some fresh air.

'We're through!' A jubilant shout from the man operating the drill brought an instant cheer from all the team. Then everyone stood back to allow Mike to speak to the boy inside the hut.

'Can you hear me?' shouted Mike, his lips as close to the drilled hole as safety would allow.

This time, the voice from inside sounded much clearer. 'Yes! I hear you!'

'Take in as much fresh air as you can. We'll carry on drilling until we've got enough room to get you out.'

The boy sounded relieved. 'Please hurry!' he called, sounding breathless. 'I don't think I can take much more of being cooped up in here.'

As soon as he had finished speaking, the frenzied activity started all over again. Piece by piece, chunk by chunk, the solid green slime was chipped away with painstaking care. Whilst it was all going on, Mike frequently looked at his watch, and wondered what the coming night would bring. Apart from the ECPU team, the beach was totally deserted, and unnaturally illuminated by the two giant arc lights, the glow of which could be seen by a crowd which had gathered on the coastside promenade just a short distance away. The lights could also be seen by a passing cargo vessel approaching from the open sea on its way upriver to London. And people on the opposite side of the Estuary were using field glasses to find out whether the lights from the Essex coast were being used for the making of a film or something. They certainly weren't natural.

After Mike had taken a turn at the drill, he wiped the sweat from his forehead and wandered down to the water's edge. It was a very dark night; the night clouds obliterated the moon and stars. There were small ripples of water lapping on the beach, caused mainly by the swell from passing boats. Normally, this was Mike's favourite view – the Thames Estuary at night, thousands of lights twinkling in the distance. But now his thoughts were on other, more dangerous things. He kept thinking about what Helen had said. Could he trust this strange 'Doctor', who seemed to come from nowhere? If what he said about the potential invasion by alien creatures from beyond Earth's atmosphere was true, would they wreak the same havoc as they had done on this very same beach? Could this be man's own fault, he wondered? Will the human race never learn to respect the ecology and natural resources of its own planet?

'OK Mike! We're there!'

Mike snapped out of his daydreams and rushed back to join his team who had finally broken a hole big enough for the trapped teenage boy to climb through.

'Out you come then!' yelled Mike through the newly made hole. 'Give me your hand, and I'll pull you through.'

Everyone waited in hushed expectation to catch their first glimpse of the poor boy who had been cocooned inside the beach hut for so many hours. But to their astonishment, there was no response. Absolute silence.

'Are you all right?' Mike called again. Still no response.

'Is anything wrong?'

The team murmured nervously amongst themselves. Had their efforts to break through into the beach hut been in vain? Had the boy, trapped in there for so long, been finally overcome by the lack of air? The men of the ECPU team waited in agony. Sweat was still running down their faces from the frenzied drilling and glare of heavy arc lights.

When there was still no response from inside the hut, Mike cautiously tried to peer through the newly made hole. But despite the arc lights on the beach, it was too dark inside the hut to see anything.

'Give me a torch, someone – quick!' he called. One of the men gave him a torch, and he switched it on. But the moment the light from the torch beam pierced the inside of the beach hut, there was a terrifying, high-pitched squeal, and something leapt straight out through the hole, knocking Mike to the ground, and scurried off towards the water's edge. As the shocked men quickly scattered in horror, they were unable to see what the 'thing' actually was. But even before Mike had the chance to pick himself up, there were more squeals and hisses, as one...two...three... a rapid succession of small, fishlike creatures came leaping out through the hole as fast as the eye could see. Soon, the entire beach was echoing to the chilling sounds of the creatures, as they darted off on clawed and webbed feet in all directions, clearly desperately making for the waters of the Estuary.

'Help me!' yelled one of Mike's men suddenly. 'Get it off me! Get it off!' He was screaming in pain as one of the aggressive fish-creatures grabbed his ankle and held on to it with tiny, razor-sharp teeth. One of the other men quickly broke off a chunk of wood from the beach-hut railings, and started hitting the creature with all his might. But the dreadful thing held on with grim determination, squealing and hissing hideously until finally it released its hold on the poor man's leg, and scuttled off to join its pack.

For a few brief seconds, the men of the ECPU team were able to get their one and only glimpse of the hideous creatures, each of them no more than six or eight inches long, who were now spread out along the water's edge, as though disoriented, not knowing what to do or where to go. They were a fearful sight as they crouched there on the shingles, eyes closed, gills pulsating rapidly, their scales not yet fully formed. But then, as though reacting to a given signal, they suddenly burst into life again, and leapt in unison into the water. In a moment, they were gone, disappearing into the dark, murky swell of the Estuary.

In utter disbelief Mike and his team watched the heinous creatures go. It was as though they had lived through a nightmare, for the appearance of the creatures seemed so unnatural, so unreal. But the man who had been attacked by one of the creatures was real enough, and so was his ankle which had been torn apart by the creature's sharp teeth, and was now gushing blood.

In the general confusion that followed, Mike was desperate to know what they would find inside that beach hut. It was incredible to believe that only a short while ago he had been listening to the voice of that boy. How did he get in there, Mike wondered. What could have happened to him, locked away with a pack of such voracious monsters?

The mystery was to remain unsolved, for when Mike finally found his way cautiously through the hole into the beach hut, there was no sign of a teenage boy or of anyone else.

What Mike did find, however, was a cluster of large, broken green-coloured egg shells.

Each one of them was empty.

Helen Briggs rowed her boat to a marker buoy which was situated in the Estuary about halfway between the coasts of Essex and Kent. She was already wearing her black rubber diving-suit, and it would not take her long to put on her face-mask, goggles, and flippers. Helen was a good underwater swimmer, but always hated using the oxygen cylinder which had to be fixed over her shoulders. At least she had found a quick way to get it on and off, she thought.

Within a few minutes of tying up the buoy, Helen was ready to go. Although it was a dark night, she could see the coastal lights in the distance and in particular the heavy glare of arc lights on the Shoeburyness beach. After checking that she had everything she needed, she carefully manoeuvred herself into place, sitting on the edge of the boat. Then she fitted the mouthpiece of the oxygen supply into her mouth, steadied herself with both hands, and finally entered the water by falling backwards with a loud splash.

On such a dark night, however, it was impossible to see the large circle of white foam beneath which she disappeared into the depths...

At a police station in London, old Ben was interrogated for more than an hour and told that until contact had been made with young Jess and Tommy, he would be treated as a murder suspect. Ben denied everything, and insisted that he hadn't seen anything of Jess and Tommy for weeks. However, when the Doctor and Sarah Jane were given an opportunity to talk with him alone, it was a different story he told.

'I was fast asleep when it 'appened,' said the old tramp. 'God knows what went on down there. All I knows is that there was this terrible din goin' on.'

'What kind of din?' asked the Doctor anxiously.

''Ard ter say. At first I thought I was dreamin'. It was this 'issing sound, went right through yer 'ead. I woke up 'cos I started ter feel the ground shakin' underneath me. I tell yer, it was peculiar. It give me the willies!'

Both the Doctor and Sarah Jane were listening intently to what old Ben had to say. There was now no doubt whatever in the Doctor's mind that the Pescaton had reached this far up the river, but what he wanted to know, and know fast, was the creature's objective. 'Tell me something,' he said urgently, standing behind Sarah Jane who was sitting opposite old Ben at the interview table. 'You say the last you saw of your two young friends was when they were down by the river's edge?'

'That's right.'

'Was that all you saw?'

Old Ben lowered his eyes. This was the part he had hoped

he would never have to answer.

'What did you see, Ben?' Sarah Jane insisted. 'You have to tell us.'

Ben's eyes remained lowered as he answered. But his voice was only barely audible. 'There was somefin' in the water down there. It come out at 'em.' His eyes suddenly flicked up, and to the Doctor. He could see the whole horrific scene was being re-enacted there. 'I never seen anyfing like that in my whole life, sir. That "thing" just come right up out of the water, and snatched 'im – just like he was a bit of cardboard or somefin'. Then it dragged 'im in the water an'... an'... I don't know what 'appened to young Tom. All I know is, I never saw no more of both of 'em, so 'elp me God.' The old tramp lowered his eyes again, and could not be coaxed out of his silence.

But just as the Doctor and Sarah Jane were about to leave the room, he suddenly turned to them with a grim-faced warning, 'Don't let anyone go in that river, sir. 'Cos if yer do, I swear ter God, yer'll never see 'em again!'

Helen Briggs swam towards the debris of the wrecked freight barge. The light from her torch threw a sharp beam into the eerie underwater dark, enough for her to find her way to the underwater cavern entrance first discovered by the Doctor. Using her flippers to guide her, Helen disappeared into the tunnel which would eventually lead her to the Pescaton spacecraft.

Not so far behind her, the water boiled and seethed. In an explosion of bubbles, there emerged the pack of small fish-creatures who had just terrorized Mike Ridgewell and his team on the Essex beach.

By this time, however, the newly-hatched Pescatons were not quite so small as they first appeared...

5

WHILE THE CITY SLEEPS

The night clouds cleared very fast, mainly because a stiff breeze had come up in the early hours of the morning. The sky was crystal clear and through the glass dome of Professor Emmerson's observatory, the Doctor and Sarah Jane could see the whole sky, dancing with trillions of stars, and a summer moon that was almost dazzling to the naked eye. But beyond the galaxies, the tiny planet of Pesca was showing signs of immense geological activity.

'I first noticed it about a couple of hours ago.' The Professor was in one of his very excited moods, and talking so fast that Sarah Jane found it difficult to follow him. 'There are so many flares on the planet, I'm absolutely certain they must be explosions of some kind.'

The Doctor had left Sarah Jane with his old friend Bud Emmerson whilst he himself returned to the ECPU base further down the Thames. Sarah Jane was furious with the Doctor for doing so, because for the past hour she had had to listen to the Professor getting more and more worked up about his new discoveries, leaving her drained and exhausted. However, if the Pescaton creature was at large somewhere in the Thames, she felt much safer on Highgate Hill.

'Have you heard of any more meteorites falling to Earth?' she asked when she finally managed to get a word in.

'So far, no, thank goodness,' replied the Professor. 'But I've put practically every observatory in the world on alert. If anything appears we'll see it, don't you worry.'

The North London Observatory was clearly Emmerson's dream come true. Morning, noon, and night his eye peered through the high-powered telescope which he had constructed with money contributed not only by astronomical organizations around the world, but also by fans of his film and television appearances. Back in the fifties, the Professor had been the first to discover a whole new cluster of planets, and this discovery had brought him instant international recognition. From that time on, his views, calculations and predictions had been avidly followed by television viewers around the world.

However, what the Professor did not know at this stage was that Sarah Jane was about to make a discovery that would far exceed any other in the history of astronomy.

'Just as I suspected,' proclaimed the Doctor, who was in the beach hut with Mike Ridgewell, examining the empty Pescaton eggshells. 'The creature they've sent is laying the first of its eggs. I have a nasty feeling they won't be the last.'

'This is an absolute nightmare!' said Mike, who was looking weary after his first encounter with a new generation of Pescaton creatures. 'When you described these "things" to me Doctor, I had no idea they were so repulsive. And what was so terrifying was their aggression. They seem to have the same instinct as some species of killer sharks: to attack on sight.'

The Doctor picked up a piece of broken shell, held it between his fingers, and examined it closely by the light of his torch. 'You're quite right, they are aggressive. Actually, the Pescatons are like a cross between two fish species which are similar to those found on this planet: the shark, which, as you know, is a seawater creature, and the piranha, a voracious river beast. It's a charming combination, isn't it?'

44

He threw the broken green eggshell back on to the floor. 'Between them, they could rip the flesh from your body in a matter of seconds.'

Mike followed the Doctor out of the hut and back on to the beach. Most of the ECPU team had now left, but the whole area was still heavily illuminated by the white glow of the arc lamps, so that as they walked, the Doctor and Mike's shadows were elongated and stretched eerily all the way down to the water's edge.

'I still don't understand how we heard that boy's voice inside the hut,' said Mike, still totally confused by all he had seen and heard over the past few hours. 'I mean, it's just incredible. We all heard it, and yet there was no one inside except those – those "things"!' He and the Doctor came to a halt at the water's edge. 'Am I going mad or something, Doctor?'

'No, my friend. You're not going mad,' said the Doctor, his eyes scanning the Estuary beyond. 'You did hear a human voice – but it wasn't coming from a human source. You see, the Pescatons are a highly developed species. They have a technological knowledge and intellect far superior to anything on this planet. Unfortunately, they have a very large, clumsy body. But their mind is quite simply brilliant. Even to the extent of assimilating sounds, analysing, and recreating them. Given the right climatic conditions, they can multiply their species in unlimited numbers.'

Mike was still peering back at the beach hut, where only a short time ago he had seen the pack of young Pescatons scurrying down to the exact spot where he and the Doctor were now standing. 'We counted ten empty eggshells in that hut. Just how many more d'you think there might be?'

The Doctor turned briefly to look at Mike. 'Who knows? Probably thousands.'

'Thousands!'

'Just remember, these creatures are fish. They can lay an endless trail of spawn wherever they choose.'

Mike was stunned as he looked around the beach apprehensively. 'You think – there are more of these

45

Pescaton eggs around?'

'I wouldn't be at all surprised,' replied the Doctor, with an all-too knowing grin.

'Then we've got to find them – destroy them!'

'That won't be easy. A Pescaton always heavily cocoons its eggs until they're ready to hatch. And once the young get into the seawater, it takes no time at all for the salt to increase their growth.'

Both men turned to stare out at the Estuary.

Far away, the small rowing boat was still tied up to the marker buoy halfway across. . .

The dark form of Helen Briggs glided through the underwater tunnel leading to the Pescaton cavern. As she went, the powerful beam from her torch picked out the clawmarks on the tunnel walls. As she entered the cavern itself, she stopped in horror and amazement, for the giant spacecraft was pulsating with a vivid emerald green colour. Treading water with her flippers for a moment or so, she tried to take in what she could see before her. Only now did she believe what the mysterious 'Doctor' had told everyone.

This was no meteorite. It was a carefully constructed space vehicle that had survived entry through Earth's atmosphere and the watery landing into the Thames Estuary. Helen reached to her shoulder strap, and unclipped the special underwater camera she had brought with her. She began to take flashlight photographs of every part of the spacecraft's exterior.

Inside the spacecraft itself, Helen began to photograph the complicated banks of controls, concentrating on close-ups of the materials used and the strange alien markings resembling ancient Egyptian hieroglyphics everywhere. When she felt she had all she needed, she reclipped her camera back on to her shoulder and made her way back through the vast spacecraft entrance.

Only then did she discover that her luck had finally run out, for the cavern outside was quite literally swamped with giant fish.

The young Pescaton predators were now almost full size.

On hearing that Helen had been seen rowing out into the Estuary wearing full diving-gear, Mike Ridgewell had rushed back to the ECPU Base, leaving the Doctor to continue his own investigations on the beach and surrounding areas. The arc lights had now been switched off, and the only light came from the moon.

The Doctor found his way to a cluster of small pleasure boats that were moored alongside a jetty, which was situated about half a mile from the beach. To his relief, he found it a peaceful scene with the brightly coloured boats bobbing gently up and down on the slight swell caused by the gathering stiff breeze. He wasn't quite sure what he was looking for. All he knew was that if the Pescaton had laid one spawn of eggs, it was almost certain it had laid more. But where? And how could the eggs be prevented from hatching?

By the light of the moon, the Doctor scoured the boats in the jetty, then returned to the beach on the other side of the walkway. His feet made an eerie sound on the hard shingles, and at times it was quite difficult to walk. It was only when he turned into a small cove and was about to climb up some narrow stone steps to the cliff above that he first heard the sound.

The Doctor stopped dead, and kept absolutely still, holding on to his hat against the wind. From the position he had reached halfway up the steps, he stared out to the waters of the Estuary which was no longer calm and restful as it had been for the past day or so. Small tufts of foam were appearing on the swell, and waves were beginning to form and crash on to the seashore. But it wasn't the sea that dominated his attention. It was something else. A sound. A sound he had heard before – a long time ago, on the planet of Pesca.

Squeals. Tiny sounds. Tiny squealing sounds. Not one of them, but hundreds – maybe thousands. All squealing together. Close by. Very close by. But where?

The Doctor slowly looked from side to side. He could see

nothing, absolutely nothing, but the Estuary, the jetty, and the beach below. But then suddenly, he saw it. Swinging his gaze upwards, he could see where the hideous sounds were coming from. Quickly scrambling up the stone steps, he arrived at the top of the cliff. And there it was.

The most ugly monstrosity he had ever seen. Towering above the clifftop like some ancient temple was a cone-shaped structure made entirely of the solid slime produced by the Pescaton. In some awful, strange way, it was a beautiful sight, silhouetted against the full summer moon, with the wind blowing, and the gathering waves crashing on to the shingled beach below.

For a moment, the Doctor made no move towards the Pescaton cocoon. He just stood there in the moonlight looking at the structure, recalling the time when he last saw such a thing. It was on the surface of the planet of Pesca, whose bleak landscape had been covered at frequent intervals by similar cones used by the Pescatons to protect their eggs until they had germinated. Slowly, the Doctor crept around the structure, listening to the squealing sounds inside that had led him to it. He estimated that there must be several hundred, probably thousands, of eggs inside, for he could hear the sounds of shells cracking, the squealing and hissing of new-born Pescatons, and the scrabbling of tiny claws tearing at the cone walls.

He knew of no way to destroy the monstrous structure and its evil occupants. He knew only too well that it would take hours to penetrate the solid slime covering the cone, and in any case it was better to play for time and leave young Pescatons where they were. But the Doctor's fear was that if he had found one such cone, where had this advance guard of the Pescaton migration formed the others? The only hope now was that when the sun came up, it would delay the young Pescatons from escaping from the cone. For the sun was their only predator. It was gradually destroying their planet, and it was their enemy.

Even as the Doctor stood there, however, cracks appeared in the walls of the cone. The occupants were beginning to emerge. Totally startled by the sudden appearance of a young Pescaton head through one of the cracks, the Doctor stumbled and found himself toppling backwards over the cliff.

To Sarah Jane's immense relief, Professor Emmerson was fast asleep. He had clearly talked himself into such an excited frenzy that he had quite literally dropped off in his chair from exhaustion whilst working out on his computer the change in activity on the planet of Pesca. Sarah Jane herself was also very tired, but there was no way she was going to get any sleep whilst being bombarded by the Professor's loud symphony of snores.

Getting up from the uncomfortable sofa where she had tried to rest, Sarah Jane made her way up to the observation platform and glanced up through the glass dome at the brilliant night sky. The stars seemed denser and brighter than ever. After being amongst them in the TARDIS so many times of late, she felt strange seeing them from her own planet again. Ever since she had teamed up with the Doctor, Sarah Jane had found it an awsome experience to travel through time and space. It was such a fantasy, so lacking in reality, that at times she felt as though she was just floating through some beautiful dream which from time to time turned into a dreadful nightmare. As she pondered the night sky, she thought about the Doctor and the enigma he was. She was only too aware that no matter how long she accompanied him as his travelling companion, she would never truly know him. But then, was there anyone who could possibly know him? The Doctor was the symbol of all that was good in life – on this planet, and throughout the galaxies.

And yet, she thought, there was a dark side to his nature. If that should ever materialize, what sort of a person would he then be?

Sarah Jane rubbed her weary eyes. Almost without thinking, she turned to the Professor's giant telescope and quite casually peered through the eyepiece. The focus had been set on the planet of Pesca, which through the lens looked about the size of the smallest coin. Although she was still half asleep, Sarah Jane looked at the view through the eyepiece and was impressed by the amazing clarity and brightness of such a huge magnification. But suddenly, her eyes sprang open. Something was happening on the planet. Huge flares pulsated constantly there, but an endless succession of small lights were streaking away from the planet and darting off into the black darkness of space.

'Professor!' She yelled out, reluctant to wake him. But what she was seeing through the telescope was too important for him to miss. 'Wake up, Professor!'

The Professor woke with a start, practically falling off his chair as he did so. 'What is it? What's happened?'

'Something's happening on Pesca,' spluttered Sarah Jane, as the Professor rushed up to join her on the observation platform. 'Take a look – quick!'

The Professor practically pushed Sarah Jane out of the way in his eagerness to get to his beloved telescope. And when he looked through the eyepiece, he felt his whole body shake with excitement. 'You're right! Exactly as I thought. The whole planet is being torn apart. Those flares – they must be explosions!'

Sarah Jane craned her head to look up through the glass dome, as if expecting to see Pesca with the naked eye. 'And can you see those streaks of light? Like shooting stars – masses of them, just pouring out of the place!'

'Incredible!'

'What does it all mean, Professor? What's going on up there?'

'I don't know. But I'll have a guess.' The Professor tried frantically to focus his lens. 'I'd say that whatever life form is on Pesca, it's doing its darned best to get away.' Then, without turning his attention away from the eyepiece, he pronounced, 'Unless I'm very much mistaken, the planet of Pesca is about to disappear from the galaxy.'

Even as the Professor spoke, he saw Pesca had become a huge white fireball, disintegrating instantly into trillions of tiny particles of light, which within seconds became tiny stars in the darkness of space.

Ashen white, the Professor turned to Sarah Jane. 'I think we'd better get hold of the Doctor,' he said breathlessly.

The Doctor clung to the small clump of tree that he had fallen on to when he fell backwards over the clifftop. Although it wasn't very far to the beach below, the shingles would have been a hard landing. Once he had recovered himself from the shock of falling, he gradually managed to pull himself upright, and after getting a firm grip on the cliff rock, he started to climb upwards.

On the clifftop the cone cracked and he heard the squeals and hisses of the cone's occupants. Feeling that he would rather break his neck than be stripped of his flesh by the newly hatched Pescatons, the Doctor began to climb downwards.

The Doctor finally dropped back on to the beach by lowering himself down from a small natural ledge cut into the rock. A short while later he was hurrying back along the coastal promenade towards the ECPU base. Before he got there, however, he saw Mike's young assistant, Pete Conway, running towards him from the beach.

'Doctor! I've been looking for you everywhere!'

'Sorry about that,' replied the Doctor quickly, trying hard to conceal a hole in the seat of his trousers, caused by his unceremonious fall into the tree. 'I'm afraid I've been delayed.'

'You've got to get back to London, sir.' Pete was still wearing his white decontamination suit, but no head cover. 'We've had a call from your colleague Professor Emmerson at the North London Observatory. He says something important's come up. It's absolutely vital you get back as soon as possible. We've got a car waiting for you.'

'I can't go until I've seen Mike. Where is he?'

Pete had difficulty in keeping up with the Doctor. 'He and the team have gone out to look for Helen,' he panted. 'Somebody saw her about an hour ago. She was rowing out into the Estuary, wearing full diving-gear.'

'What?' The Doctor came to an abrupt stop. He was horrified. 'Doesn't she realize what's going on out in that water?'

'I know, Doctor. But you don't know Helen. Once she sets her mind on something, no one can stop her.'

Mike, wearing rubber diving-suit, goggles, and flippers, leapt into the sea from the ECPU motor launch. He had a full cylinder of oxygen, enough for about half an hour searching the Estuary bed close to the marker buoy where Helen had tied up her small boat. Remembering what had happened to the previous ECPU diving team who had gone searching for the fallen submerged meteorite, Mike's team begged him not to enter the dangerous waters of the Estuary. But, although Helen was obstinate and sometimes too self-willed for her own good, she meant a great deal to Mike and he was determined to go after her.

The seabed of the Estuary was surprisingly cloudy, and even with his underwater torch Mike had difficulty in finding his way around. But eventually he reached the wreckage of the old freight barge, and from there on he persevered until he caught his first glimpse of the tunnel which led to the Pescaton cavern. For a brief moment he paused at the tunnel mouth, reluctant to enter. But it seemed the logical thing to do so, like Helen a short time before him, he used his flippers to float gently forward.

Once inside the cavern itself, Mike made quite sure that he moved cautiously. He was absolutely staggered to find the huge spacecraft there, and genuinely frightened by the dazzling emerald green light emanating from it.

Like Helen and the Doctor before him, Mike found his way into the spacecraft. He searched quickly around it and got out again as fast as he could. By this time he was feeling very pessimistic about the chance of finding Helen alive for, even without the danger of an encounter with the Pescatons, she could not possibly survive without oxygen. It was only when he was about to leave the cavern that he noticed something tucked away behind the spacecraft that intensely intrigued him.

It was a small cone-shaped structure, formed out of the same kind of material as the solid green slime Mike had seen cocooned around the beach hut. He swam closer, and with his torch, prodded the side of the cone. To his astonishment, it moved slightly, and after using all his effort to push at it, the cone toppled over.

Helen, only half conscious, was still alive, the mouthpiece of her empty oxygen cylinder still clamped to her mouth.

Mike moved fast. Guessing that Helen had survived only because the cone had served as an airlock, he took a quick deep breath, pulled out Helen's mouthpiece and inserted his own. Then, supporting her beneath her shoulders, he used his flippers to get them both out of the cavern as fast as possible.

Back in the tunnel again, Mike paused briefly to give himself another lungful of oxygen. He breathed deeply, then returned the mouthpiece to Helen, whose eyes were only half open behind her goggles. It was only when the two divers were heading out of the tunnel entrance that Mike suddenly realized they were being trailed by the pack of young Pescatons.

He made a wild dash for the surface. But Helen was a dead weight and with their amazing speed of movement in the underwater depths, it took no time at all for the Pescatons to surround them.

It was a terrifying moment for Mike, for he was now quite certain that both he and Helen would be torn to pieces by the voracious creatures. For what seemed like an eternity, the newly hatched Pescatons floated menacingly all around their prey. It was as though they were waiting for Mike and Helen to make the first move. But, to Mike's astonishment, the aggressive pack suddenly darted off as quickly as they came, and disappeared back into the safety of their own cavern.

A few minutes later, Mike and Helen were at the surface again, and quickly picked up by the jubilant ECPU team on board the motor launch.

At Professor Emmerson's observatory, the Doctor and Sarah Jane watched a video replay of the extraordinary disintegration of the planet Pesca. But what the Doctor was really interested in were the streaks of light that had shot out of the planet and headed into space.

There was now no doubt in his mind that the full Pescaton migration had begun.

One by one, the blinding 'meteorites', dropped into the murky waters of the Thames Estuary, dazzling the great City of London.

6

THE TERROR BEGINS

At first light the following morning, the city of London was calm and peaceful. In Trafalgar Square the pigeons had not yet descended on the tourists for their daily feast of birdseed and titbits, and the early morning rush hour was only just beginning to build up. Further along the river, however, it was a different picture.

Ever since the 'meteorites' started dropping into the dark waters of the Thames, it seemed as though the entire world's press had descended on the Essex and Kent shorelines overlooking the Estuary. Television cameras were there to relay live reports back to the early morning breakfast shows, newspaper photographers had hired boats to take 'exclusive' pictures of the river area where the 'meteorites' had dropped and anyone who looked even remotely official was interviewed for their reactions. Everyone agreed, it seemed, that this was the greatest phenomenon to occur since Galileo first discovered that the planet Jupiter had satellites.

At the ECPU base headquarters, Mike Ridgewell was inundated with requests for interviews, but his superiors at the Department of the Environment in London had instructed him to say nothing about Helen's encounter with the young Pescatons on the bed of the Estuary. There was no doubt, however, that Helen's survival in the airlock of the underwater cone was nothing short of a miracle. Recovering in the ECPU first-aid unit, Helen explained that after the Pescaton creatures had surrounded her, they had systematically formed a cone of slime which had immediately solidified around her. When this had been done, the water inside the cone was extracted, and she was left with enough air to survive until Mike had rescued her. For Helen, it had been a nightmare experience. She had felt like a fly trapped in a spider's web. The puzzling question that still remained, however, was why the young Pescaton creatures didn't tear her and Mike to pieces on sight.

Within a few hours both shorelines of the Estuary had been sealed off from the public, and during the course of the morning the beaches on both sides of the Estuary were crowded with Ministry and local government officials, observers and analysts from environmental groups, and amateur astronomers desperate to get a glimpse of the fallen 'meteorites'. In fact, most of them were so intent on concentrating their attention on the Estuary itself that they hadn't yet noticed a much more sinister phenomenon which had appeared on and around the cliffs near Shoeburyness.

It was a group of towering cone-shaped structures, formed of solid green slime.

The Doctor and Sarah Jane hadn't slept much that night. Ever since Professor Emmerson had passed on the news from his overseas colleagues that 'meteorites' were falling into rivers and oceans, not only in the British Isles but also around the world, they had been searching the banks of the Thames all the way from the Tower of London to Richmond. It was an utterly exhausting, frustrating job for both of them, because even if they did come on any of the Pescaton creatures, there would be very little they could do to stop them wreaking havoc everywhere. Already the multiple landings of the Pescaton spacecraft had caused the levels of the river water to rise dangerously, and a huge wave had swept its way in from the Estuary causing flooding right into Berkshire. It was late afternoon before the river once again returned to its normal calm, allowing a clutch of sailing boats to take advantage of the breeze.

'Stupid idiots!' snapped Sarah Jane as she watched the coloured sails of the small boats passing back and forth along the river. She and the Doctor had picked up the first signs of the green sticky substance, which led to the towpath alongside the Thames at Richmond. It was a hot summer evening, and people were flocking out of their offices and homes to take in the last of the day's sunshine. To them, the news reports of 'meteorites' dropping into the Thames Estuary down river seemed to be pure science fiction with absolutely no relation to their own lives. So they carried on exactly as they would on any other normal day. 'Don't they realize they're putting their lives at risk out there?'

The Doctor was scanning the river through his own personal pocket telescope. 'How can you tell people their lives are at risk from something they don't even know about?'

'Then they should be told. If only the television and newspapers could tell the truth for once, instead of making it all up as they go along.'

The Doctor turned to look at her and smiled. 'Well, you're a journalist or something, aren't you?'

Sarah Jane turned to look at the Doctor, and as soon as she'd taken in what he'd said, she chuckled. 'You're right. I hadn't thought about that.'

Just at that moment, they were distracted by a commotion coming from a pleasureboat which had moored alongside a small island midstream. The boat was full of tourists all pointing and taking photographs of something which was causing a great stir.

'What is it, Doctor? Can you see?'

The Doctor, peering throught his pocket telescope again, suddenly became very excited. 'This way! Hurry!'

Without another word, he suddenly grabbed Sarah Jane's hand, and rushed them both off towards a riverside jetty, where he quickly hired a rowing boat.

A few minutes later, the Doctor and Sarah Jane had tied up on the small island, which was thick with trees and other foliage. Despite the warning notice which read '*NO LANDING*', they quickly jumped on to the sloping grass bank, and stood looking at the cause of all the commotion.

Sarah Jane stared in shock disbelief. 'I don't believe it! It – it's absolutely horrible!'

Laid out in the woods in a perfect triangle, were three Pescaton cones, all constructed from their solid green slime.

'Move on!' The Doctor was shouting at the top of his voice to the skipper of the pleasureboat. 'There's nothing to see here!' he yelled, waving his arms wildly. 'Move on!'

The pleasure-boat passengers waved back at him, and hurled abuse, telling him to 'Push off!' or 'Who d'you think you're talking to!' But the skipper of the boat seemed to be convinced that the Doctor was some kind of official from the River Authority, so he quickly started up the boat's engine again, and headed off back to Westminster Pier.

Once they had gone, the Doctor and Sarah Jane moved in for a close inspection of the cones. To the Doctor's surprise, there was no sound of squealing or hissing coming from inside the cones. The Pescaton eggs would probably start to hatch as soon as it got dark.

'They're extraordinary,' whispered Sarah Jane, almost too scared to speak. 'Why do the Pescatons build these terrible things, Doctor? What do they use them for?'

'They use them to protect their young,' replied the Doctor, his voice also low. He was moving from one cone to another, putting his ear against them to see if there was any sound of movement coming from inside. 'You must remember, Sarah Jane – the Pescatons are fish. They either spawn their eggs in water, or some place protected from the sun and the planet's atmosphere.'

'They hatch all on their own? Without help?'

'Oh yes.' The Doctor turned only briefly to look at her. There was a grim expression on his face. 'And much faster than any fish species here on Earth.'

'Right! Who's responsible for this, then?'

The Doctor and Sarah Jane turned with a start. Approaching them from a motor launch on the other side of the small island was an officious-looking middle-aged man, wearing a pinstriped suit and thick, hornrimmed spectacles. Behind him came a team of labourers, all wearing protective helmets, and carrying heavy sledgehammers, pickaxes and drilling equipment.

'Was it you?' sniffed the little man, who had to stare upwards in order to look at the Doctor's face. 'Are you the one who's dumped all these things here?'

'I have nothing to do with it,' replied the Doctor, stone-facedly shaking his head.

'Then what are you doing here?'

'Official business. What about you?'

'Mr. Potterton. Thames River Authority.' Feeling into the top pocket of his jacket, the little man whipped out a plastic identity card, showed it quickly under the Doctor's nose, then put it back into his pocket again. 'This island is our property, and you're trespassing.' Then he turned and glared straight at Sarah Jane. 'Both of you.'

Sarah Jane glared back scornfully at Mr. Potterton. He was her least favourite type of person, and she'd met his sort many times before in her job. 'We have as much right to be here as you,' she snapped. 'As a matter of fact, we're from the Department of Environment,' she sniffed haughtily. 'The Doctor and I are carrying out some research here.'

'Are you now?' Potterton flicked her an ingratiating smile. 'Then where's your ID card?'

Sarah Jane was about to argue, but the Doctor interrupted quickly. 'No point in hanging around here any longer, Sarah Jane.' They turned to leave, but the Doctor noticed the team of labourers setting to work on one of the Pescaton cones. Rushing over to one, who was wielding a huge sledgehammer, he said urgently, 'I advise you not to do that!'

The labourer paused a moment, and waited for Potterton to join them. 'Take no notice of him!' he snapped, his hornrimmed spectacles practically steaming up with indignation. 'Just carry on.'

The Doctor was now angered by Potterton's arrant stupidity. 'If you break into any of these cones, you'll — you'll . . . all I'm saying is, you'll be making a big mistake.' Staring straight at the little man, half pleading, half demanding, he said, 'I'm warning you now. Don't stay on this island after dark. Leave the cones alone.'

They left and walked to the boat. The last thing they heard as they rowed back to the towpath jetty, was the sound of drilling and hammering.

An hour or so later, the sun finally set over the small island in the middle of the Thames.

As night returned, the stiff breeze turned into a gusting wind, and, thanks to those uncaring passers-by who had no interest in using the public litter bins, the streets of London quickly became alive with old discarded newspapers, empty Cola tins and takeaway packets which floated and bounced along the pavements with alarming animation. Dustbin lids blew off and clattered into back yards. Stray cats yowled tetchily, and no self-respecting mouse dared venture out of its hole in such weather.

In all the parks, tall trees creaked and swayed precariously in the wind. Ducks, wild geese, and all kinds of birds sought sanctuary in their usual safe hiding places, and even the cocky London sparrows had more sense than to search for a late-night crumb of bread. In Hyde Park, old Ben had taken refuge in a rowing boat alongside the Boat House. But he got very little sleep, for the water in the Serpentine Lake was churned up by the gale-force wind, and the little boat was tossed about mercilessly. During the summer months, Hyde Park was one of Ben's favourite kipping places, for he could always find somewhere to hide after the park gates had been shut to the public. Thanks to the Doctor's intervention, he had been released from police custody, when it was decided that there was no way in which he could have been implicated in the disappearance of his young companions. However, from that moment on, old Ben had vowed that he would never kip down beside the river again.

Highgate Woods were also being ravaged by the wind. Grey squirrels burrowed deep into the earth for protection, and the fish in Highgate Pond remained perfectly content in the comfort of their pond weed. The window-shutters at the North London Observatory rattled noisily in the gale. Although most of the other residents in the area had turned in for the night, the lights were still blazing away in the Observatory and even from a distance Professor Emmerson could be seen through the glass dome, peering eagerly through the eyepiece of his telescope.

'We must find a way to destroy those eggs before they hatch! If we don't, the consequences are too fearsome to imagine.' The Doctor's voice echoed around the glass dome, as he anxiously paced back and forth on the wooden tiled floor of the Observatory. 'The Pescatons are going to colonize not only this country, but also practically every other corner of the planet as well.'

'Why don't they burn the little blighters?' As he had had another sleepless night, for once the Professor wasn't talking quite so fast. 'Drill a hole in one of these cone things, and spray them with flame-throwers.'

The Professor's suggestion sent a cold chill down Sarah Jane's spine. 'How horrible!' she said with a shiver.

'I'm afraid it wouldn't work, Bud,' replied the Doctor. 'From what I can remember when I was on the planet of Pesca, the creatures can resist any form of combustion.'

As he spoke, the Professor's telex machine burst into action by his desk on the other side of the hall. The Professor rushed across to collect the message. 'Two more "meteorite" landings,' he read out. 'One in the Zambezi in Africa, the other in the St Lawrence just outside Montreal in Canada.' Scratching the thinning hair on his head, the Professor looked up. 'That makes thirteen sightings around the world so far. Looks like we're in for a glut of fish,' he remarked wryly.

Sarah Jane finished her cup of tea and leaned her head back wearily on the sofa. 'There must be something we can do to stop these awful creatures. We can't just let them take over like this.'

61

The Doctor went to the window, and stared anxiously out at the storm clouds racing across the dark night sky. 'Every creature has its own predator,' he said, half to himself and with just a shred of optimism. 'Let's hope the Pescatons meet theirs very soon.'

The storm clouds were also gathering over the Thames Estuary, where the world's media, together with the police and countless officials from all sorts of National and Local Authority Departments, were joined by a team of divers from a Royal Navy destroyer, now anchored close to the position where the 'meteorites' had landed. But the surface of the water was much too rough for the diving team even to contemplate an expedition to the depths. Apart from the high wind, which caused the destroyer's bunting to flap violently, it was raining hard, and every small boat in the vicinity was having a tough time avoiding capsizing.

Wearing yellow oilskin hoods, jackets, trousers, and heavy gumboots, Mike Ridgewell and his young assistant, Pete, searched the shoreline for any further sign of Pescaton activity. Struggling against heavy wind and rain, they finally reached the spot where the Doctor had found a green solid-slime cone on the clifftop.

There was a whole cluster of cones on the beach and more on the clifftop itself. All of them had great cracks in the walls where they had been broken open.

Inside the cones were dozens of Pescaton eggshells. Each one was empty.

Several miles upriver, on the small island at Richmond, the sound of high-speed drilling and hammering had to compete with that of wind and rain. But despite the strenuous efforts made by the team of labourers, the cones remained stubbornly intact. It was a frustrating, bewildering, and tiring task for them all, made worse by the constant harassment by Mr Potterton, the little man from the River Authority.

'It's no use!' yelled Derek, the foreman, rain pelting down onto his helmet and face. 'There's no way we're going to get into these things. The only thing that'll move 'em is dynamite.'

'Keep trying!' bawled Potterton, from the shelter of his umbrella, which had already blown inside out at least half a dozen times. 'I want them all off this island by daybreak!'

'I'm telling you – it's impossible! God knows what they're made of, but we can't even touch 'em'

'Derek!'

Derek turned with a start to find one of his men calling to him from one of the cones. He rushed across to the man who had his ear pressed up against the wall of the cone.

'There's something inside. I can hear it.'

'What?' Derek wiped the rain from his face, then pressed his own ear up against the cone wall. The expression on his face was a mixture of astonishment and apprehension.

'What's going on?' Potterton approached. His hornrimmed spectacles were like drenched car windscreens.

'I don't believe it,' replied Derek. 'Just listen to this.'

Potterton took off his spectacles, and pressed his ear up against the cone wall. Gradually, he could hear it. The squealing. The hissing. Movement. Impatience. 'What the hell? There's something sealed up in there.'

By now, all the men had their ears pressed up against the cone, and as the rain pelted down on to their faces, a streak of lightning in the sky was followed immediately by a vicious clap of thunder. There was fear in all the men's eyes. But they didn't know why.

Potterton suddenly pulled back from the cone wall. 'Get back to work – all of you!' he yelled. 'Let's get these things opened up!'

A few moments later, the men continued their work with renewed vigour, determined to get inside the cone and release whatever it was that was trapped there. Potterton made his way back to the shelter of the River Authority's motor launch which was moored close by. From there he spoke by radio with his headquarters and assured them that he had everything under control and that he would have all the cones dismantled before morning. True enough, even while he was speaking, Derek the foreman called him back. A small crack had at last appeared in the cone. Potterton hurried back to find that the men had managed to wedge a heavy chisel into the crack and were gradually succeeding in widening it.

Whilst all this was going on, the rain continued to pelt down as the gale brought down chunks of dead branches from the trees above. As they toiled away, however, the men did not notice the turbulence in the river behind them. The surface of the water, already distorted by the constant downpour of rain, was now swelling dangerously, causing the motor-launch to break its mooring and drift away. The water became rougher and rougher until a huge whirlpool formed alongside the island.

And then it happened. Just as the men had succeeded in breaking open a large chunk of the cone wall, the sound of wind and rain was completely overwhelmed by a roaring, hissing sound, and suddenly the whole island was bathed in a dazzling emerald green light. Out of the river came the Pescaton creature, rearing up like an angry serpent, claws gleaming in its own light, and eyes piercing straight across the tiny stormswept island.

For a moment, the men were paralyzed with fear. All they could do was to stare at the monstrous sight before them, their faces bathed in the emerald glow from the creature's massive body.

'For God's sake!' yelled Derek. 'Let's get out of here!'

The labourers scattered in all directions, but were horrified to discover that the motor launch had already drifted away from the island and was rapidly disappearing downriver on the fast-flowing current. Only one person was left behind. Potterton, still clutching his half-wrecked umbrella, was dazed into immobility. As the towering Pescaton roared down on to him, his thick horn-rimmed spectacles reflected the whole grisly scene right to the very end.

Another streak of lightning flashed across the sky, closely followed by a loud clap of thunder.

The explosion of sound was immediately taken up by the deafening roar of the Pescaton creature which stomped across the tiny island, tearing down every tree in its path. The men screeched and screamed. With nowhere to go, they rushed around frantically, like frightened animals hunted by their predator. In sheer panic, some of them leapt into the raging river water. It was their final mistake.

A short while later, human bones floated downriver on the racing current.

By the time the Doctor had heard about the horrific events on the island, the Pescaton had already emerged from the river and was rampaging through the streets of London. Suddenly, lights were glowing in every home in the city. The Prime Minister was woken up, and immediately called an emergency meeting of his Cabinet. The media flocked to cover the phenomenon, and, in an attempt to block the creature's path, the police and army brought in reinforcements. But despite the fact that the alien creature was wreaking havoc in its path, the order to destroy it was witheld in the absurd hope that some way could be found to capture it alive.

The Doctor and Sarah Jane caught up with the Pescaton as it retreated into a canal and trudged its way clumsily through water far too shallow to submerge its immense size.

'Where's it going to, Doctor?' Sarah Jane had to shout to be heard above the excited yells of the crowd who were following the destructive creature at a safe distance behind. 'What's it trying to do?'

'I'm not sure,' the Doctor called back. 'But I've got a feeling it's searching for something.' For the past ten minutes or so, the Doctor had noticed that the Pescaton was moving at a more sluggish pace. Although it had continued to tear down telegraph poles and wires as it went, this had been more because of clumsiness than anything else. But it was still a deadly and ferocious creature, and anyone who ventured too close to it, or tried to take flashlight photographs, risked a swift and violent end.

Further along the canal, the Pescaton appeared to find what it was looking for. It had reached the outer fence of the

London Zoo, where the roar of animals inside caused it to respond with a weird, angry, squealing wail of its own. The Doctor was now watching the Pescaton with intense interest, for there was no doubt that it was getting weaker by the minute. However, it still had enough strength to smash down the perimeter fence, and it was here that the crowds were allowed to follow no further.

Once inside the grounds of the Zoo, the police and army were given orders to bring the Pescaton down with tranquilizer pellets. But this proved to be an utter failure, for the pellets were totally incapable of penetrating the steel like surface of the creature's scales. However, the Pescaton was now getting noticeably weaker, and as it lumbered its way towards the Aquarium Halls, the police immediately threw a cordon around the place. There was a great deal of consternation from Zoo officials as they watched the massive creature smash its way through into the Aquarium Halls building, and they were sure that they were about to lose their collection of precious marine life.

Suddenly, an ominous silence fell over the Zoo. There was no sound from any of the animals at all, not even from the screeching monkeys, trumpeting elephants, or bad-tempered lions. Everyone was puzzled, especially the Zoo officials, who although used to contact with the most bizarre of exotic animals, had never before seen anything quite like the voracious creature now ensconced in one of their Aquarium Halls.

The high wind and rain had at last stopped, and it would not be long before the sun started to rise over the adjoining Regent's Park. In the eerie silence that had now overwhelmed the Zoo, everyone watched and waited for the Pescaton's next move.

The Doctor signalled to Sarah Jane to follow him. Making quite sure no one was watching them, they found their way around the back of the Aquarium Halls building, and slipped in through a side door.

One part of the vast building was still intact, and as there were no windows, the Halls were in darkness except for the rows of glass tanks that were illuminated day and night by heavy light bulbs. The Doctor moved cautiously through the small hall. Sarah Jane followed him reluctantly, feeling almost sick at the sight of the vast array of marine creatures who were watching with large glaring eyes from either side.

'Doctor!' Sarah Jane was so nervous she found herself hardly able even to whisper. 'I really don't think this is a very good idea.' As she spoke, she passed a large glass tank where the eye of a massive octopus seemed to be staring straight at her. 'These things don't look very friendly.'

The Doctor didn't answer. His attention was too drawn towards the damage in the large Main Hall beyond, where the Pescaton had broken in, and where the first streaks of daylight were beginning to filter through from the half-demolished roof above.

Slowly, but cautiously, the Doctor and Sarah Jane approached the large main hall of the Aquarium. There was debris from the glass tanks everywhere; the floors were swimming with water, and marine life of all shape, colour, and size were flapping around helplessly, desperately struggling to survive. Only one enormous tank was left intact, and this contained two agitated sharks who looked as though they would much rather be back home in their natural hunting grounds, the deep coral reefs of Australia.

As they drew closer to the hall, the Doctor held up his hand and brought Sarah Jane to a halt. 'Keep absolutely still,' he whispered. 'Leave this to me.'

For a few moments, they waited in silence. But whilst they did so, there came a weird sound from inside the main hall. It was the sound of the creature, hissing with what seemed like no energy at all. And it could be heard breathing – slowly, deeply, and intermittently. The Doctor poked his head slowly around the open arch of the hall.

Peering in, he caught his first glimpse of the Pescaton. It was crouched on all fours, on its claws and webbed feet, looking like a giant lizard perched on top of a rock, and absolutely motionless except for the signs of breathing, which seemed to show mostly from the sack of skin beneath its throat.

The Doctor stared at the creature in absolute astonishment. 'It's incredible!'

Sarah Jane, keeping well out of sight behind, became impatient. 'What is it, Doctor? What's going on?'

'The Pescaton,' he called, without turning back to her. 'Something's happening to it. It – it's losing its energy.'

'Losing its energy? What are you talking about?'

'Its eyes. They're different. They've changed their colour. The body... that's different too.'

Sarah Jane was utterly bewildered, and tried to take a sneaking look herself into the main hall. But the Doctor kept her back.

'No, Sarah Jane! It's not safe – not yet. Leave this to me.'

'No, Doctor!' Sarah Jane tried to hold him back. 'It's far too dangerous. Don't go in there – *please*!'

Obstinate as ever, the Doctor ignored her and slowly crept into the main hall of the Aquarium. It was an awesome sight, with broken glass and dying fish everywhere. But as he approached the recumbent creature, the Doctor was acutely aware that the sun was just beginning to rise; its first rays were now streaking through the half-demolished roof at the far end of the Hall. The Pescaton was now breathing faster and more frequently, and as it breathed, it seemed to emit a low growling sound, rather like a dog. But even though the Doctor was now only a few feet away, the massive creature still did not react.

The Doctor edged forward cautiously, astonished to see that the creature was totally transformed. It had lost its green luminous glow, its eyes were shut tight, and the scales covering its body were no longer shining. Could it be, he thought, that what he was witnessing were the dying moments of a Pescaton? And if so, why was it happening?

As he moved closer, however, the creature's eyes suddenly sprang open, and the familiar laserlike beams tore into the Doctor, sending him reeling to the floor on the other side of the Hall. Simultaneously, the creature let forth a roar that caused the entire Aquarium building to shake to its very foundations, bringing more debris in its wake.

'Doctor!' Sarah Jane's terrified shout echoed around the Aquarium halls. Defying the Doctor's instructions, she rushed to his assistance, and quickly tried to pull him out of the path of the suddenly active Pescaton. 'Doctor! Are you all right? Oh, please say you're all right!'

The Doctor had merely been stunned, and was able to recover immediately. 'That'll teach me to take a Pescaton for granted,' he muttered wryly.

As the Doctor spoke, there were renewed growling sounds from the other side of the Hall. He and Sarah Jane turned, to find the creature becoming more and more agitated. Only then did the Doctor realize what was happening. The sun! The Pescaton's one and only predator, the reason why their entire race was migrating. The sun was burning the planet of Pesca right out of the galaxies.

During the moments that followed, the Doctor and Sarah Jane were joined by a stunned group of Zoo workers and policemen. And as all eyes turned to watch the Pescaton, the sight they witnessed was a truly incredible one.

There was now complete silence throughout the Aquarium building. The Pescaton, looking like some huge dinosaur, its tail stretched out straight behind, was now completely still. Not a sound, not a movement came from the enormous beast. Its breathing had stopped altogether, and although its eyes were open, they were fixed and glazed like marble.

'It's dead,' cried one of the Zoo workers.

He started to venture towards the creature. 'No – wait!' the Doctor called out.

The sun's rays had finally reached the centre of the Main Hall, and were now shining directly on to the Pescaton. Then, as everyone looked on in stunned disbelief, the creature's scales started to steam and hiss. The fumes were so pungent that everyone started to cough and splutter, and as the steam gradually cleared, all that was left before them was the skeleton of what could have been some large prehistoric monster.

After the initial few moments of shock, the Doctor and

Sarah Jane were the first to go forward to look at the skeleton of the creature.

'It's incredible, Doctor!' croaked Sarah Jane, still hardly able to speak after the sight she had just witnessed. 'It disintegrated – right before our very eyes. That really is the end of the hideous thing. The end of the Pescatons forever!' Suddenly feeling brave again, she reached out her hand to touch the bones. As she did so, however, the whole body collapsed, causing her to scream out in terror, and leap straight into the Doctor's arms.

The Doctor smiled comfortingly at her. 'Not quite the end, Sarah Jane.' Then his expression changed as he turned to look back at what was left of the Pescaton. 'As a matter of fact, I think this is just the beginning.'

7

PESCA

As expected, it took only a short time for news, photographs, and television pictures of the extraordinary death of the Pescaton to be flashed around the world. In New York, the United Nations met in emergency session, and for once agreed unanimously that the world's oceans, rivers, and lakes should be searched without delay for Pescaton spacecraft. An International Scientific Commission was immediately set up to investigate and analyse any information that was provided by conservationists and environmentalists around the world, and each country was assigned the task of keeping a close watch for any more 'meteorite' sightings.

Whilst the people of London gradually took in the fact that they had been subjected to an onslaught by a bizarre creature straight out of science fiction, a twenty-four hour watch was put on the Thames all the way from its source, in Gloucestershire, to its Estuary on the North Sea.

On the clifftops at Shoeburyness, the Doctor, Sarah Jane, and Mike Ridgewell examined the cluster of Pescaton cones. Every one of them were now cracked wide open, and the eggs inside were empty.

Wearing protective gloves and an anti-pollution mask

around his mouth, Mike was collecting some of the broken eggshells. 'You know, Doctor,' he said, popping them into a plastic bag for examination later by his own forensic experts, 'it scares the wits out of me that these things are just swimming around in that water out there.' He tied a knot in the plastic bag, then lowered it carefully into a thermosealed box. 'D'you think they really will start attacking soon?'

'I don't think there's any doubt about it.' replied the Doctor, who had discovered the young Pescatons' trail of solid green slime leading from the cones straight down into the sea. 'Unless I'm very much mistaken, the Pescatons are massing together in every ocean, river, and lake around this world. It's only a matter of time before they start to move.'

'But how do we know they haven't all died off?' called Sarah Jane, squatting on one of the stone steps which led down to the sea. 'Just like that awful creature in the Zoo last night.'

'No chance of that, I'm afraid,' insisted the Doctor. 'What we saw last night was a renegade Pescaton which was foolish enough to expose itself to the sun's rays.'

Sarah Jane looked puzzled. 'But why did it trudge all away across London to the Zoo? What was it searching for?'

'Various things. These creatures have developed an uncanny sense of smell. They can detect anything miles away. But my guess is that it was after the salt water in the Aquarium.'

'Salt?'

'There's not enough salt in the Thames water to keep them alive for too long. That's why they're massing together in the Estuary. It's much closer to the sea.'

Mike turned to look at the Doctor, who was now staring out towards the sea. 'I don't understand. If these Pescaton things are intending to attack, what are they waiting for?'

The Doctor paused before answering. 'The signal,' he said at last.

'Signal?'

After the violent storm of the night before, it was now a

hot afternoon again, and the sun was shining out of a brilliant clear blue sky. 'Mike,' said the Doctor, taking off his hat briefly and fanning himself with it, 'I think you should know that this planet is on the brink of colonization by one of the most ferocious invaders mankind has ever had to face. But not one of these devils are allowed to think for itself.' He hesitated only long enough to put his hat on again. 'In my opinion, one of the reasons why you and Helen were not torn to pieces during your dive the other night, was because those young Pescatons were under "instructions" not to touch you. If they're going to survive on this planet, they're going to need all the human brainpower they can assimiliate.'

For a moment, neither Mike nor Sarah Jane could speak. What the Doctor had said seemed so utterly wild and crazy that Mike found it impossible to believe. But in the short time he had known the Doctor, he had learnt that anything he said was based on sound logic.

'Instructions, Doctor?' Mike asked. 'Whose instructions?'

The Doctor did not answer. He was standing on the edge of the cliff, staring out in deep thought towards the sea. There was a grim expression on his face as he watched the small tufts of foam curl over the surface of the sea. And above it, that vast expanse of sky that led to the great beyond in time and space – his home. And as he stood there, with a gentle summer's breeze brushing against his face, he felt as though he was floating in air... on... on... until his mind gradually travelled back to that extraordinary moment in his long life, when the TARDIS was drawn into the magnetic field of a dying planet that was Pesca...

For thousands of years, Pesca had been rich in vast oceans and continents. Bright yellow and orange soil, green grass, lush valleys, and high mountains with huge rock formations. But as the sun drew closer and closer into the planet's orbit, the deep blue waters of the Pescan seas were drying up.

The Doctor stepped out of the TARDIS to find that it had landed on a huge dried up salt-water lake. As he walked, he could see the bones of what had clearly once been fish of all

73

species, and the soil on the bed of the lake which was now hard, almost like rock, and parched white by the intense rays of the sun. The landscape itself was one vast desert, scorched to destruction over a relatively short period of time, and now totally uninhabitable.

Every so often, the Doctor would come across remains of former Pescaton civilizations, strange underwater caverns that must have once been the hub of daily life amongst the marine population. And all around the banks of the dried-up lake there were dozens of weird, cone-shaped structures, once bright green but now a pallid yellow and with no sign of having broken open to release its newly born occupants.

But as the Doctor toiled aimlessly on his way, the same question crossed his mind time and time again. How did it all happen? And why did it happen? As he travelled throughout space, the Doctor had often heard it rumoured that the Pescatons were an avaricious species which had plundered the natural resources of their planet to such an extent that nothing was left. And by using substances that were harmful to the atmosphere, the population had destroyed the protective ozone layer above their planet, leaving it exposed to the penetrating ultraviolet rays of the sun.

With no shade from the intense heat of a Pescan day, the Doctor felt stifled and desolate, as though he was the only living thing on the entire planet. His only thought now was to return to the TARDIS and get away as fast as he could. But, as always, his curiosity got the better of him. He just had to see more, he had to know if this bizarre civilization had really come to an end.

His exploration led him to what had obviously once been a wide stretch of river which curved across a lifeless plateau for miles into the distance. The area where the TARDIS had landed was fairly mountainous, so he decided to climb a little in order to get the best view he could of the surrounding terrain. On the way, he noticed the extensive lava formations, which immediately told him that Pesca was not only mountainous, but also volcanic. Everywhere, great streams of molten rock had set hard and were pitted with the remains of marine life, preserved for as long as the planet would survive.

When he had reached a high vantage point, the Doctor was able to get a true picture of the doomed planet. Although he had caught a brief glimpse of the terrain in his video monitor during the last few moments of descent in the TARDIS, it was nothing to the reality of actually seeing the entire dead landscape laid out before him.

Most of all, it was the silence that disturbed him. On any other planet, especially Earth, it would have been a great blessing, but here it was joyless and unreal. No sound of the wind blowing through trees, no birds to sing, and no wild beasts to roar or screech their presence from a lush green jungle. For even before it had died, Pesca had been the habitat of nothing more than creatures of the sea and rivers and lakes. Oh, how the Doctor wished he could hear the magical sound of running water, the sea smashing against rocks, or a waterfall, endlessly racing over the edge of a cliff into a lake below. But as he stood there, perched like Moses on the pinnacle of a huge protruding rock, surveying his kingdom laid out before him, that unnatural silence came to an unexpected end.

In the distance he could hear activity of some kind. At first, he thought he had imagined it, but as he concentrated hard, his ears gradually became attuned to the sounds – mechanical and electronic sounds, bleeps and humming. From his jacket pocket, the Doctor quickly took out his Dynameter, which looked like a thermometer, and was his own device for tracing sonic direction. Holding the gadget above him, he was soon able to discover the source of the sounds he was hearing.

Within a short while, the Doctor had found his way to the slopes of what had once been a small active volcano. But when he eventually reached the summit of the crater, he was surprised to find that it had been capped with a mushroom-shaped structure made entirely of a green solid-slime substance. Upon further investigation, however, the 'mushroom' was found to be a huge electronic covering device which could be raised or lowered as necessary.

So there was still a life force of some kind on the planet.

Using the Dynameter the Doctor crawled about the slopes of the volcano, his ear pinned to the solid lava, listening to the frenzied activity in the depths below. Somewhere, thought the Doctor, there had to be an entrance to the volcano. But where? As he looked around for some crevice or hole which might lead him into the crater, he was unaware of the sinister infrared periscope that had emerged like a cobra from the rocks behind him.

His every move was being watched.

Edging his way flat on his stomach around the uppermost rim of the 'mushroom', the Doctor felt the hardened lava suddenly give way beneath him, open up and send him reeling into a vast chasm below.

Down... down... down... The Doctor seemed to be falling through the dark for he knew not how long. All he knew was that, as he fell, his body was turning over and over, utterly out of control, and yet somehow weightless in the stifling atmosphere of the endless chasm.

It was some hours before the Doctor regained consciousness, and when he did, he wasn't sure if he was dead or alive. For a short while his eyes felt too heavy to open, so he just lay there, listening to a distant sound that he never expected to hear on the planet of Pesca – the sound of a waterfall. He tried to move his hands. His entire body also felt heavy, as though he had been paralyzed by an injection of some tranquilising substance. But he felt no pain. This puzzled him, for he had fallen from a great height, and even a soft landing would surely have caused some injuries.

There was another sound close by. As yet, he couldn't tell what it was. But he knew it was there. He felt its presence strongly. Something breathing. Something... hissing! Still, he couldn't open his eyes. Gradually, he was able to move his lips and croak just a few words.

'Who's... there? Who... are you?' No reply. No physical contact. 'What ... do you want ... of me?'

76

As though suddenly released, the Doctor's eyes sprang open and to his horror he saw what was towering over him. During all his years travelling through time and space, this was the most hideous and gigantic form he had ever seen. A massive creature, with slanting, luminous green eyes bulging out of an oval head covered with shining, metallic scales. Its teeth were sharp and pointed, like needles, and the gills behind its head pulsated as it breathed. And the body! The fins of a killer shark, hands with sharp claws, and the legs of a human stretching down to veined webbed feet. The creature's tail, which was long and tough, like that of a crocodile, stretched out behind its body but never seemed to move.

The Doctor had no idea if the creature had any means of communication, but he summoned up all the energy he had left to repeat this question 'What . . . do you want . . . of me?' he croaked breathlessly. 'Tell . . . me.'

As the creature bent its huge head down towards its helpless captive, the Doctor was transfixed by its eyes. They were clear, like glass, and a bright green. And through those eyes the Doctor could see right inside the creature's brain, a hideous mass of living energy, a great beehive shape, crawling with minuscule 'thought worms'. It was absolutely horrible.

'I am Zor, leader of all Pescatons.' The creature could speak, he thought. 'We have been waiting for you, Doctor. We knew you would come.'

The Doctor could hardly believe his ears. This hideous monstrosity, half fish, half human and with the face of the devil himself, was actually speaking words in a human language. But even more horrifyingly, the creature's voice resembled that of the Doctor himself.

'What . . . do you . . . want of me?' The words tumbled out breathlessly as he tried to restore some life back into his hands. 'I . . . I can't move!'

'You are our prisoner, Doctor.' The Pescaton Leader spoke with no emotion whatsoever. 'You will help us.'

'No one can help you.' The Doctor tried to blink his eyes, but he realized that every part of his body was being controlled by his menacing adversary. 'Don't you know your planet is dying? The sun is burning you right out of the galaxies.'

Every time the Doctor spoke, Zor's own voice picked up the identical speech and tone patterns. 'That is why you will show us to our new world. You will save us, Doctor. You *will* save us!'

'New world? What are you talking about?' The Doctor's whole body system suddenly felt as though it had received an electric shock, for not only did his speech immediately return to normal, but he sat up sharply without any effort from himself. Only at this moment did he discover that he had been lying stretched out on a circular slab of a stone he had never seen before. Looking around, he saw that he was prisoner in a vast subterranean cavern bathed in a dazzling emerald-green light. Hanging from the ceiling and from the rough-hewn walls were stalactites which looked like giant green icicles formed out of volcanic lava and slime. And beyond the cavern, the Doctor could see the waterfall he had heard, tumbling down into what looked like the shore of some vast underground lake.

Zor raised itself up to reveal its enormous height. 'We shall use your special powers to find a planet where the sun can harm us no more. The Pescaton civilization must not die.'

'You think so?' said the Doctor facetiously. 'And how do you Pescatons intend to survive when there's hardly enough water left to fill a tea cup?'

The Doctor felt the electric shock vibrate through his body again, and suddenly, in the split-second blackout that followed, he was transported to the shores of the lake beyond the cavern. The lake was more like a great ocean, and stretched as far as the eye could see. It was rather beautiful, with the gush from the waterfall tumbling down the subterranean walls into the calm, salt waters of the lake. In fact, the only thing to mar the grandiose view were the clusters of huge, solid, green slime cones that lined the shores of the lake, casting their reflection on the surface of the water everywhere.

78

The Doctor turned to Zor, who had clearly used the same transportation device to re-materialize at the Doctor's side. 'Why d'you want to leave a lovely place like this?' he asked. 'As a matter of fact, I wouldn't mind a bit of a swim myself.' It was a remark he wished he hadn't made, for the calm waters of the lake became suddenly rough and turbulent, and within seconds the surface was crisscrossed by what seemed like hundreds of sharklike Pescaton fins. The Doctor swallowed hard. 'Oh well, I'm not a very good swimmer anyway,' he spluttered.

Zor's long tail swished back and forth slowly for the first time. 'The Pescaton civilization is the most advanced in the entire cosmos.' And by the perfect way in which the creature spoke, the Doctor believed it. 'Our race is prepared for the great migration. Soon, our machines will be ready to transport us.'

'Machines?' The Doctor was stunned. 'You have machines that can travel through space?'

Once again, the Doctor felt the electric shock vibrate through his body, and in the black-out that followed he had materialized into the vast space of the volcano's crater. Before him now was a sight that stunned him. All around, for as far as the eye could see, were hundreds and hundreds of replica TARDIS telephone boxes, all the same colour and bearing the same legends as the Doctor's. The only difference was that each TARDIS replica was at least four or five times bigger than the original.

The Doctor immediately rushed from one replica to another, peering inside each of them. But the contents he found caused him to burst into wild laughter, for the interior of each TARDIS contained nothing more than a police telephone. 'You really expect your entire race to migrate from this planet in these things?'

Zor was not amused. 'You will help us, Doctor.'

'Don't be ridiculous!' The Doctor was unable to contain his laughter. 'What you've built there is a police telephone box. You wouldn't even get the thing off the ground!'

As the Doctor continued to rock with laughter, Zor kept

repeating, 'You will help us. You will help us.'

Finally, the Doctor composed himself. 'I'll do nothing of the sort,' he snapped, firmly. 'You Pescatons have brought about your own destruction through evil and greed. Even if I could help you, I wouldn't!' He stepped up to Zor, glared right up at the huge creature defiantly, and said 'Just know this, my friend. There's only one TARDIS. And that's the way it will always be.'

He hardly finished when the electric shock shot through his body again and he found himself lying back on the stone slab in the cavern, unable to move his limbs.

'You will help us, Doctor.' Zor was hovering over the Doctor again. This time, the light from the creature's emerald-green eyes was almost unbearable. 'You will help us!'

'No! Never!' The Doctor, now only just able to move his lips tried hard to close his eyes. But whatever hypnotic power it was that Zor was using to control the Doctor's movements, the Doctor's eyes remained firmly open. 'I... will not... help you,' he struggled to say. 'I will ... never... help... you...'

'The eyes, Doctor. The eyes. Tell me what you see...'

'No!'

The massive frame of the creature drew closer and closer to the Doctor, and as it spoke, the scales on its arms glistened like a million stars. 'Tell me... Tell me what you see...'

It was now impossible for the Doctor to resist the mental pressure. As he stared into Zor's piercing eyes, he could see the hideous minuscule 'thought worms' scrabbling around in the creature's brain. They appeared to be tiny particles of organic matter which formed part of Zor's internal computer. But the creature's eyes told the Doctor far more. They were a metaphysical mirror in which so much of the Doctor's life and former existence was reflected. Flashing before his eyes were his countless journeys through time and space, the planets and galaxies he had passed through, his companions, friends, and foes. He could see himself tumbling through space, turning over and over and over, as if in slow motion, ageless through time. But no image was free of Zor,

Leader of the Pescatons, the cruellest race throughout the cosmos.

For what seemed like an eternity the Doctor lay there, with Zor's voice – his own – tearing into his mind, commanding him to help and to obey. And gradually, the Doctor felt his life ebbing away from him. There seemed no escape from Zor's powerful computerlike brain, which was clearly the nerve centre of the entire Pescaton species. Locked in a frenzied mental battle, the Doctor was also coming under its control, for the mighty Zor was attempting to absorb the Doctor's knowledge of the galactic universe and the immense solar system beyond. However, the Doctor's resistance finally proved more than the Pescaton leader had bargained for, and the creature was no match for the Doctor's strength of mind with which he had been gifted throughout his many generations.

The Doctor's eyes suddenly sprang open with a start. Zor was no longer hovering over him. And his body – now it felt different. He tried to move his toes. They wiggled without effort. He felt his fingers scraping the stone slab beneath him. Could it be that Zor's mental power had at last been broken? For a moment he just lay there, trying to refocus his mind after the intense strain of his struggle with the Pescaton Leader. It was then that he felt a strange sensation. There was something on his stomach ... crawling... slowly... The Doctor raised his head slightly, and looked down. But for a moment he found everything blurred, until gradually, he saw it, crawling up his chest, and only an inch or so away from his face. A crustacean – a huge red coloured crab, with claws that were raised, and poised for battle.

The Doctor leapt up with a jolt, sending the huge crab tumbling with a thump to the hard lava floor. The Doctor looked around the cavern. It was a sight of nightmarish horror, for the entire cavern was crawling with crustaceans of every shape, size, and colour – thousands of them, a great seething mass of hard-shelled creatures covering the floors, the walls, and even the rock-structured ceilings. The cavern was one great moving army of shells. Perhaps these poor creatures are also the prisoners of the Pescatons, thought the Doctor. As he watched the crawling mass in horror and disbelief, he soon realized how the dominant species of the planet were satisfying their voracious appetite.

He looked around for a possible means of escape. He knew that once he reached the surface, the Pescatons would not be able to follow him. But it was not going to be easy trying to walk over a floor crawling with crabs, and cross a lake full of Pescatons. Suddenly, he remembered the waterfall. Surely there would be a means of escape there – at the source of the water? Somewhere? Quickly putting on his hat, which had been tucked crudely into his jacket pocket, the Doctor took a deep breath, and jumped down on to the floor.

Most of the crabs scattered in all directions, but one or two raised their claws, and opened them defiantly. His slow walk became more of a shuffle, and occasionally he had to brush off one of the smaller crabs which was tugging at his trousers. Slowly but surely, he made steady progress towards the waterfall beyond the cavern. By the time he got there, he had left most of the crustaceans behind, and his last view of them was of thousands of claws raised high, almost as if wishing him good fortune.

Thankfully, the surface of the salt-water lake was calm, with no sign of Pescaton activity anywhere. But he knew only too well that they were never too far away, and that Zor, their leader, was probably watching every move he made. The waterfall itself seemed to be gushing down from between two rocks in the wall high above the lake. But at the side of one of the rocks, the Doctor was encouraged to see what looked like a narrow crevice which might possibly lead to the surface. He had never considered himself a good climber, so he was dreading the thought of the journey up. However, tucking his trousers into his socks, and pulling his hat firmly onto his head, he entered the waterfall, and started climbing precariously up the rock-face just behind it. It was a slow and laborious task, but he made quite sure that he got a firm grip on any lump of rock available that would help lever him up to the crevice.

The lake below suddenly came alive with activity. Dozens of young Pescatons emerged from the water and tried to leap up towards where the Doctor was climbing behind the waterfall. Throwing caution to the wind, the Doctor quickened his pace, and within a few more minutes, he was standing on a ledge beside the two rocks between which the water was gushing. Then, taking a final glance down at the frustrated creatures hissing and growling at him from the lake below, he quickly disappeared through the crevice in the rock wall.

The crevice was dark and narrow, but the Doctor was able to ease himself up a little at a time by keeping his back to one wall whilst treading his feet against the opposite wall. But eventually his efforts were rewarded when he saw light filtering through a gap near the apex of the crevice.

It took almost an hour before the Doctor found his way onto the surface again, but when he did eventually get there he was even grateful to feel the burning hot sun on his face. He had emerged from a completely different part of the volcano slopes from that which he had entered, so he was able to make his escape with much more ease and speed.

A short while later, the Doctor was back in the TARDIS again – the real TARDIS, he thought to himself, his TARDIS. Once inside, he immediately turned on the video monitors to check that his departure would be without hindrance. With great relief, he had not been followed as he had expected, so he set about activating the TARDIS control systems.

The dematerialization process was not functioning. No matter what programme he tapped into his computer, there was no chance of an immediate escape from the parched planet on to which he had been drawn.

The scaled face of Zor appeared on all his video screens. 'You will help us, Doctor,' boomed the voice of the Pescaton leader. 'You will help us!'

'Never!' yelled the Doctor in great fury. Wrestling frantically with the TARDIS controls, the Doctor realized that Zor was once again trying to use hypnotic telepathy to hold on to him.

For minutes that seemed like hours, the Doctor was locked in mental battle with the leader of the Pescatons. Using the video screens as their point of contact, the two minds struggled for supremacy. But just when the Doctor felt that all life was ebbing away from him again, the TARDIS controls suddenly burst into life, and the image of Zor on the video screens rapidly broke up.

Within seconds, the TARDIS had dematerialized, and as the Doctor watched the parched landscape of the dying planet gradually disappear from his video screens, he had a nasty feeling that this would not be the last time he would see the Pescatons.

At least, the Doctor thought, the Pescatons would not be travelling anywhere in their police telephone boxes.

8

CREATURES OF THE NIGHT

After the intensive wave of 'meteorite' landings, an uneasy calm had settled over the rooftops of London. The government had declared a state of emergency, not only in the capital, but throughout the United Kingdom. There had been meteorite sightings in the Lake District, the Scottish Lochs, the Avon Estuary in the West Country, and in all coastal areas, so from now on no chances were to be taken. For the time being, boat traffic was banned from all rivers, and the skippers of fishing trawlers were warned to keep a constant lookout for any sign of the alien invaders.

The rest of the world too was on a high state of alert. From the United States to Africa, from Asia to the South Pole, there were reports that during a period of twenty-four hours, 'meteorites' were seen dropping into rivers, lakes, and seas with alarming regularity. In Japan, a Buddhist monk described how he had seen a dazzling bright light streaming down from the night sky only to crash with a spectacular explosion into the slopes of Mount Fuji. Since then, however, there had been an ominous silence.

All the world could do was to wait.

'But how soon will the Pescatons get this signal, Doctor?' asked Sarah Jane as she and the Doctor made their way across Hampstead Heath on their way to meet Professor Emmerson. 'And where will they get it from?'

The Doctor's long legs were striding at a fast pace across the grassy heath, making it difficult for Sarah Jane to keep up. 'From the central nerve system of their energy source. Their leader, Zor.'

'Zor?' Out of breath, Sarah Jane stopped walking, to rest for a moment beneath a huge oak tree. 'What's that?'

The Doctor stopped and turned. Then taking his hat off to fan himself, he described his visit to the planet of Pesca way back in the Earth time of the fifteenth century. Even though the sun still had an hour or so to set, it was a warm evening, and there were quite a lot of people around taking advantage of a last-minute stroll.

Sarah Jane listened to the Doctor with awed fascination. This was the first time he had talked about Pesca and his extraordinary encounter with Zor. 'You mean, this creature can control the movement of every single Pescaton? The whole lot of them?'

'That's about it,' replied the Doctor.

'But by now there must be thousands of them in rivers and lakes and oceans all over the world. And if they keep spawning eggs everywhere, there could be millions of them.'

'I'm afraid that's what we're up against, Sarah Jane.' Arms crossed, the Doctor leant against the tree. In the distance he had noticed a group of schoolkids playing football. One of them was sitting on the banks of the pond, feet dangling in the water, adjusting the sails of a rather splendid-looking model boat. 'Zor's brain is virtually a computer, far in advance of any technology here on Earth. No Pescaton is ever allowed to think for itself.'

'What happens if it does?'

The Doctor turned to look at her and drew his finger across his throat.

'How horrible!' So many things were going through Sarah Jane's mind. The thought that all Pescatons were under the control of one leader, that they could assimilate the voice and vocal mannerisms of a human and then reproduce it, as Mike Ridgewell had found out when he and his men had tried to break in to one of the Pescaton cones on the beach. 'I still don't understand why they should choose to come here,' she pondered. 'I mean, there are so many other planets they could have gone to.'

'Water,' the Doctor answered immediately. 'There are probably more oceans, rivers, and lakes on this planet than anywhere else. And quite a lot of other natural resources they could do with too.'

'Yes. Give them half a chance and they'll blow our world to pieces, just as they did with their own planet.'

'Precisely. But it's not only water and other natural resources the Pescatons are after. It's knowledge. Our friend Zor has quite a voracious appetite for it.'

Sarah Jane turned with a puzzled look. 'Knowledge?'

'If they're going to survive on Earth, they have to know a lot more about the place. If I know Zor, he's already seeking out the best human brains he can find.'

'And what about everyone else?'

The Doctor turned to her with a wry smile. 'Pescatons have to eat, you know.'

They began to make their way past the pond on the Heath and the Doctor stopped briefly to talk to the young boy with the model sailing boat. He was particularly impressed by the unique design of the boat, which contained many advanced features for something that was, presumably, bought as a toy.

'That's a fine boat you have there,' said the Doctor, crouching down to take a closer look. 'Where did you get it from?'

'I made it myself.' The boy's reply was delivered in a confident voice. He was aged about fourteen, a bright-faced kid, who wore metal-rimmed spectacles, a black school blazer, and grey flannel shorts. 'I always make my own boats.'

Sarah Jane was also impressed with the boat. 'Not much wind today though. She won't get very far.'

The boy looked indignant. 'My boat doesn't need wind.

It's got a built-in remote-controlled motor.' Without any more discussion, he waded into the water until it came up to his knees, then used a small remote-control unit to start the motor. In a few seconds, the boat was gliding smoothly away down the pond.

'Excellent!' exclaimed the Doctor. 'Well done.'

The boy ignored him, and continued to watch his invention as it disappeared almost out of sight.

'Bright kid,' remarked Sarah Jane as she and the Doctor continued on their way across the Heath.

'Yes,' replied the Doctor. He said nothing more until they reached Professor Emmerson's laboratory.

The Thames Estuary was bathed in a deep crimson glow, and as a flock of seabirds headed inland for the night, their silhouettes quivered against the eerie haze of the sun slowly dipping into the sea.

It had been over a week now since the 'meteorite' phonemena had hit the world's headlines, and an air of complacency had fallen over London. As a helicopter infrared scan had shown no trace of either Pescatons or their spacecraft on the bed of the Estuary, the Home Secretary had withdrawn the massive police watch on the river. And despite heated warnings by Mike Ridgewell, the Departments of Defence and the Environment prepared for a joint underwater search, which would be carried out under the protection of the Royal Navy. But restrictions were not yet lifted on river traffic, so it was more with despair than in shock that through the window of the ECPU building, Mike caught a glimpse of a coal barge, chugging its way up river from the Kent side of the Estuary.

'ECPU One to Coast Guard 340. ECPU One to Coast Guard 340. Come in, please. Over.' Mike, using his binoculars to peer at the freight barge through his office window, was trying to make radio contact with the Estuary Coast Guard two miles away.

Mike got an almost immediate response. 'Coast Guard 340 to ECPU One. Coast Guard 340 to ECPU One. What's up,

Mike? Over.'

'That damn fool coal barge.' Mike's voice was urgent and near hysterical. 'Doesn't he know there's a Prohibition Order on the river? What the hell's he doing out there? Over.'

'Take it easy, Mike. It's only old Jock Langton. He's on his way up to Battersea to deliver an urgent supply. We got him special clearance. Over.'

'You're crazy!' Mike was practically yelling into the radiophone. 'That water's full of those damned things. They're killers, Dave. They could attack at any time! Over.'

Dave, the Coast Guard radio operator, was clearly embarrassed by Mike's hysterical outburst. 'Look, Mike. Nobody's actually seen any of these – whatever you like to call them. Not in this part of the river at least.' He chuckled awkwardly. 'Most of us are beginning to think they're a bit of a joke. I mean, let's face it, the weather's been terrific these past few days, and we haven't even caught a sight of one of them. Over.'

Mike was beside himself with frustration. 'Don't be such a fool, Dave!' he yelled. 'Don't you realize these things are creatures of the night. They never appear during daylight! Over.'

'Well, mate – it's nothing to do with us. We've got clearance for the barge. As far as we're concerned, that's it. Over and out.'

Through his tannoy speaker, Mike heard Dave break radio contact. Then he angrily threw the *OFF* switch of his own transmitter. 'Stupid, idiotic prats!' he growled to himself.

Jock's coal barge was just disappearing in the distance, heading serenely towards the Pool of London.

The sun had now set over Hampstead Heath, and all that was now left was the last of the lingering twilight. Most of the evening strollers had made their way home, leaving only a few squirrels, mice, and rats to roam the undergrowth unchallenged. Occasionally an owl hooted or a dog barked, but apart from the distant rumble of traffic, the rapidly approaching darkness was being greeted with a fair amount

89

of respect. The crescent-shaped moon had already risen, and was so bright that it cast a dazzling white reflection on the surface of the pond. The pond itself had provided enough pretty postcard views for passing strollers. Now, like everything else, it was ready to retire for the day.

The boat's engine purred quietly across the surface of the pond, the moon embracing its white sails, so that they stood out like ghosts dancing on the water. Although the Heath was now deserted, the young boy, who made such an impression on the Doctor earlier in the evening, was still there, knee deep in shallow water, watching and waiting patiently as his prized creation obediently returned to him. All around, the profusion of trees looked down, their leaves and branches forming sinister patterns and shapes against the crescent moon. But young Martin was unaware of anything but the vast galaxy of twinkling stars crowding every corner of the sky above. They seemed to be telling him something, to be warning him. It was a warning, however, that he was not prepared to accept. And as the bright crescent moon cast a flood of light on his fresh young face, the surface of the pond before him shimmered, and gradually a ring of bright water became a whirlpool. Martin lowered his eyes to watch. He was not afraid.

With a deafening roar, the Pescaton reared up out of the water, flooding the pond with its luminous green glow. Towering menacingly above the small human shape, at first it seemed that the creature would strike immediately. But, as if obeying a command, its roar became nothing more than a snarling hiss and it remained quite motionless, its webbed feet firm on the muddy bed of the pond. After a moment of silence, its emerald-green eyes suddenly came to life, and pierced the moonlit night with two laserlike beams directed straight towards his prey.

Young Martin, still clutching his model sailing boat, stared back at the creature. He was not afraid.

'Can't understand it,' snorted the Professor, as usual peering through his telescope. 'Why should the Pescatons want to migrate to Venus as well as Earth? I mean, fish can't survive in an atmosphere that's full of carbon dioxide. There's not even a drop of water vapour on the entire planet.'

'I disagree, Bud,' replied the Doctor who was at his old friend's side, looking up through the glass dome of the Observatory at the dazzling bright star that was Venus. 'As I remember, Venus has some rather large oceans.'

Professor Emmerson immediately turned from his telescope. He was at his most indignant. 'Rubbish! The place is nothing but a desert wilderness. It's a world where life of any form has never developed.'

'Wrong again, I'm afraid. The last time I was there, I discovered that the oceans contained primitive creatures not unlike the Pescatons, which are similar to those you had in your own seas here on Earth more than five hundred million years ago.'

'Professor, I'm confused,' called Sarah Jane from the hall below the observation platform. 'Are you saying some of the Pescatons landed their spacecraft on Venus, as well as Earth?'

'I'm not sure if they actually landed,' said the Professor, leaving his telescope to come down the steps into the hall. 'But unless my calculations are wrong, just before the disintegration of Pesca some of those "meteorite" lights certainly headed off in the direction of Venus. Whether they actually landed or not is a matter of opinion.'

'Renegades!' called the Doctor, his voice echoing around the Observatory.

The Professor looked back up at him. 'I beg your pardon?'

The Doctor leaned over the rails to call down to the Professor. 'If any of the creatures broke away from the mass exodus of migrants, my bet is that they would have done so as an act of defiance.'

'Goodness!' Sarah Jane was only half joking. 'A Pescaton that thinks for itself. Now there's a turn up for the books.'

The Professor was clearly becoming irritated by the conversation. There was nothing he hated more than being proved wrong. For years he had studied the endless constellations through his telescope, and regardless of the fact that human knowledge of the planets was rapidly increasing by the use of manned and unmanned space probes, the Professor considered his own views unchallengeable. 'Well, I just wish these damned fish things would hurry up and show themselves,' he grunted. 'Wipe out the lot of 'em, I say. Get the country back to normal.'

'I'm afraid it won't be as easy as that, Bud.' The Doctor looked through the telescope himself. 'The Pescatons are a superior race. They're a force to be reckoned with.'

'Rubbish!' growled the Professor. 'That's exactly what Hitler said during the war. We soon dealt with him, and we'll do exactly the same with these – these fish things. For God's sake, man, we are British, you know.'

'Good for you, Professor!' Sarah Jane chuckled for the first time. She had taken a great liking to the delightfully eccentric, but utterly endearing Professor.

'By the way, Bud,' called the Doctor, still peering through the telescope, 'd'you know anything about that young lad who builds his own model boats? Sarah Jane and I met him down by the pond on the Heath. He seems quite bright.'

'Young lad?' The Professor tapped away at his computer. 'I don't know any young – oh. You mean Martin? Martin Wilson? Lives with his aunt on the other side of the Heath. I know her well. The boy's parents died in a car crash soon after he was born. Yes, he is a bright lad. Quite exceptional, I'd say.'

The Doctor turned round from the telescope and looked down. 'Exceptional? In what way?'

'I hear he's got a very high IQ. There's talk of him going to university at least two years early.'

The Doctor was deep in thought. He was beginning to look anxious again.

'Actually, it's funny you should ask,' continued the Professor, aimlessly tapping out the keys on his computer.

'Why?'

'Well, I had a telephone call from Mrs Wilson just before you arrived. She wondered whether I'd seen anything of Martin. Apparently the boy hadn't got back home.'

Now Sarah Jane was looking concerned. 'But it must be pitch dark on the Heath by now. He can't still be out there?'

'I hope not,' sniffed the Professor. 'It's not at all safe for anybody to be out on that Heath after dark.'

Without saying another word, the Doctor leapt down the steps from the observation platform, and rushed out the door.

'Doctor!' Sarah Jane yelled. 'Doctor! What is it?'

She hurried after the Doctor along the winding path across the Heath. Not far behind them, wielding his faithful umbrella as a potential weapon, followed the Professor.

During a heated late-night debate in the House of Commons, the Opposition were lambasting the Home Secretary on his hurriedly prepared proposals to deal with any future Pescaton attack. Whilst each Member spoke, no one heard the shrill call of a tug horn from the river outside.

Jock Langton's coal barge was making good progress up river. She had already passed beneath Westminster Bridge and the Members' terrace of the House of Commons, and fairly soon she would pass beneath Lambeth and Vauxhall Bridges before reaching her final destination at Battersea.

Jock was very proud of his barge, which he had called *Pretty Sally*, after his wife. He had bought her nearly ten years before, when he had started a small business carrying supplies of coal by river from the distribution depot on the Kent side of the Estuary to Battersea Power Station. Although *Pretty Sally* was looking a little shabby these days, Jock had kept her in immaculate mechanical condition, and was determined to hold on to her for a couple more years, or at least until he retired. That night, Andy, one of his four sons, had come along for the ride, but as usual he had been no help to his father and had spent most of the journey stretched out in the back of the boat, listlessly dangling his hand in the water.

'Andy,' called Jock from the steerhouse. 'I've told ye not to put your hand in that river. Ye never know what's lurkin' down there.'

Andy laughed. 'Och, don't be so stupid, Pa!' Even though his eyes were closed, he was wide awake. 'This is not Loch

Ness, y'know. Londoners dinna have enough imagination to invent a monster in their river.'

'Dinna ye believe that, ma boy!' Jock left the wheelhouse for a moment or so, and made his way carefully along the inner ledge of the barge to check the water levels from up front in the boat's bows. 'I've been hearing some pretty weird tales this past week or so. They say there are creatures in this river that could tear the whole of London to little pieces!' He checked the gauge, then lowered it overboard again. Looking ahead, he saw that the barge was now halfway between Lambeth and Vauxhall Bridges. 'I'm tellin' ye, I wouldn't be out here tonight unless I had to!'

A loud splash come from the rear of the boat. Turning with a start, Jock saw that Andy had disappeared.

'Andy!' he yelled in panic at the top of his voice. Hurrying as fast as he could back along the ledge, he reached the bench where Andy had been stretched out. 'Andy! Oh no!' Then quickly leaning over the back of the boat, he desperately tried to look for his son. There was no sign at all. 'Help!' he yelled, as loud as he possibly could. 'Somebody ... help me!'

There was a sudden roar and the gigantic head of a Pescaton reared up from the water.

Jock's blood turned to ice.

He fell back into the boat in horror as the creature hacked its way into the vessel, lifting it right out of the water, scattering coal everywhere, and snapping the old barge in half as though it were nothing more than a fragile matchstick.

All that was left now of the *Pretty Sally* was the driftwood that floated downriver. Within a few moments the waters of the Thames were whipped into a frenzy, as the creatures of the night finally emerged to start their great onslaught on the capital city of London...

By the light of a torch, the Doctor and Sarah Jane picked their way through the undergrowth on Hampstead Heath. Professor Emmerson stumbled along just behind them, his huge frame only just visible in the dark. Overhead, the crescent moon had temporarily disappeared behind a thin veil of cloud, and by the time they had reached the pond everything was just a dark and eerie silhouette.

'Doctor, do be careful,' whispered Sarah Jane, making sure she held on tightly to the Doctor's jacket. 'Whenever we go searching around in the dark, there's always trouble.'

'I still don't see what all the fuss is about,' snorted the Professor, biting hard on his unlit pipe. 'Young Martin's a sensible lad. By now he's probably sitting at home working on some new invention.'

'Let's hope you're right, Bud,' replied the Doctor, slowly casting his torch beam over the surface of the pond. 'But I very much doubt it.'

The Professor took a handkerchief out of his pocket and, to Sarah Jane's consternation, blew his nose loudly. 'It all sounds a bit far-fetched to me. I mean, even if there are any of these fishy things in that pond, why should they go for a young lad like Martin?'

'Because they need him, Bud. Or rather, they need his mind.'

There was a sudden movement in the water. The Doctor immediately turned off his torch. 'Ssh!' he whispered. 'Don't anyone move!'

For several minutes they waited in the dark. In the distance, they could hear a cat howling. Clearly the wretched thing was trying to lure some unsuspecting mouse from its hole. But there was no further sound from the pond itself, and when the Doctor turned the torch on again, he found that a small piece of dead branch had fallen from a tree above into the water just in front of them.

'We're wasting our time,' grumbled the Professor. 'It's obvious the boy's not here. For goodness sake let's go back home and I'll telephone his aunt...'

Even as he spoke, Martin's distant voice pierced the darkness. 'Help me... please! Somebody help me!'

The Doctor, Sarah Jane, and the Professor all turned at the same time. But when the Doctor tried to shine his torch in the direction of the boy's voice, the battery suddenly gave out and they were plunged into the dark again.

'Please!' young Martin called over and over again. He sounded truly desperate and very frightened. 'If you're there – please help me!'

The Doctor, Sarah Jane, and the Professor were looking from one side to another, but without any light they felt totally disoriented. Eventually, the crescent moon emerged from behind the obstinate cloud again.

It revealed a sight which chilled everyone's blood.

No more than a hundred metres from where they were standing, there was a clearing in the woods. And in those woods, reflected in the bright moonlight, they could just see a cluster of hard green slime cones.

'Hurry!' The Doctor rushed off.

'No, Doctor!' called Sarah Jane. 'It's too dangerous. Remember what happened on the beach.'

The Doctor ignored her and headed off towards the woods.

'Help me! Please – hurry!' Martin's anguished calls immediately persuaded the Professor to follow the Doctor. Reluctantly, Sarah Jane joined them.

The Doctor soon located the cone from which young Martin's voice seemed to come. He quickly searched around for something – anything – that could be used to break into the cone. But he knew only too well that it was an impossible task; the solid slime walls were almost impenetrable.

Sarah Jane was frantic. 'Doctor, what are we going to do? There can't be any air inside that thing. He'll suffocate!'

The Professor was making some kind of a contribution by poking angrily at the cone with his umbrella. 'Martin!' he yelled. 'Can you hear me? It's Professor Emmerson. Don't be frightened. We'll get you out of there.'

'Hurry, Professor! Hurry!' Coming from inside the cone Martin's voice sounded muffled.

'For the time being, there's nothing we can do.' The Doctor was anxiously circling the cone, examining every bit of it. 'We'll have to leave him here. We have no choice.'

'But if we leave him here, he'll die!' Sarah Jane was kicking the wall of the cone in anger and frustration. 'Oh God! I hate the Pescatons! I hate them! There must be something we can do.'

Realising that Sarah Jane was losing her nerve, the Doctor quickly grabbed her by the shoulders and shook her. 'Sarah Jane – listen to me. There is nothing we can do! Even if we could get into the cone, it's just possible that it wouldn't be young Martin we'd find in there. The Pescatons could be playing a trick on us.'

The Professor turned to the Doctor in near disbelief. 'A trick? What kind of trick?'

'The Pescatons have the ability to assimilate the human voice and brainpower. It's just possible that they want us to believe that Martin is inside that cone. It's also possible that the cone is full of the creature's eggs!'

'Professor!' cried Martin again. 'What are you waiting for? Why don't you hurry?'

'We're coming, Martin! We're coming!'

A terrifying, familiar sound pierced the calm night air.

'Doctor!' Sarah Jane screeched as everyone turned towards the pond.

One by one, the creatures emerged from the pond, roaring and hissing as they came, flooding the woods with the dazzling green glare of the Pescatons as they slowly made their way towards their cones and the three helpless humans who were now at their mercy.

9

'FIND ZOR!'

Professor Emmerson never knew he could run so fast. At school he had been a terrible athlete, and much preferred browsing in the library. But at the age of sixty-four, he had suddenly discovered his feet, and even more important, how to use them. However, if it hadn't been for the Doctor and Sarah Jane dragging him away from their encounter with the Pescatons on Hampstead Heath, he might have still been there. For a time, the Professor, refusing to be intimidated by the 'fishy devils', had stood his ground, challenging them with his umbrella. Eventually, of course, survival took precedence over pride and his hasty retreat seemed to have been completed in less time than it took to run a four-minute mile!

By the time the Doctor, Sarah Jane, and the Professor had reached the safety of the Observatory, television news flashes were reporting the Pescaton 'invasion' of the Thames. The destruction and havoc the creatures were causing in adjoining districts was enormous. London had seen nothing like it since the Blitz, and every available police officer and soldier had been brought in to contain the alien terror.

The Doctor was particularly concerned about Sarah Jane.

Usually she was a tower of strength, and never gave in easily to fear, but the Pescaton encounter on the Heath had truly unnerved her. 'You mustn't give in, Sarah Jane,' he said, trying to comfort her. 'We'll win this fight, just like we won all the others. You'll see.'

'That's all very well,' replied Sarah Jane, uncharacter-istically close to tears, 'but we've never had to face anything like the Pescatons before. How are we possibly going to destroy creatures so much stronger than us?'

'Bullies never win, Sarah Jane. No matter how big or strong they are!'

In the background, the Professor, was speaking on the telephone to young Martin's aunt. He was trying to sound bright, but even he was finding it difficult.

Sitting beside Sarah Jane on the sofa, the Doctor lowered his voice and said, 'Now listen to me, Sarah Jane. We've been together some time now, you and me. We've had some exciting adventures, and some difficult ones. But we've never lost faith. Now try to remember that. Promise?'

Sarah Jane looked up at him with her large brown eyes. 'Promise,' she whispered. And managed a smile.

The Professor finished his telephone conversation, and came across to them. 'Poor Mrs Wilson. She's out of her mind with worry. Apparently Martin didn't go back home after school. He's never done such a thing before.'

'I'm not surprised,' replied the Doctor. 'He's never come under the influence of the Pescatons before.'

The Professor scratched his cropped hair. 'You really think that's what's happened?'

'I have no doubt whatsoever.'

Sarah Jane looked up. 'Doctor, are we really going to leave that boy to die out there?' she asked feebly.

The Professor was angry again. 'Don't you worry, my dear. Once they get the Army out on that Heath, they'll blast those fish things right out of the pond! We've dealt with far worse things in our time, I can tell you!'

The Doctor smiled wryly to himself. He admired his old friend's guts, but not his solution to the problem.

'And what about all those people in London?' Sarah Jane asked. 'The Pescatons are going to annihilate them. They're going to annihilate the whole world.'

'No, Sarah Jane.' The Doctor had a strange expression on his face, as though he was having one of his inner conversations. 'The Pescatons are not going to annihilate the whole world.'

'Then who's going to stop them?'

'I am.'

Both Sarah Jane and the Professor looked up with a start. 'You?' said Sarah Jane. She had seen that strange look on the Doctor's face many times before, and now felt the first sign of hope. 'How, Doctor?'

'By finding their leader, Zor.' The Doctor got up from the sofa, and went to the window to look out at the skyline of London in the far distance. It was clear that the Pescaton attack was now fully underway, for there were fires burning everywhere. 'You see, the Pescaton creatures are like railway carriages without an engine, a clock without its mechanism, or even an ordinary torch without batteries. They cannot exist without power. And that power is Zor.'

He turned from the window to look at Sarah Jane and the Professor who were watching him in awed fascination. 'If we are to destroy the Pescatons, we have to destroy that power!'

Excited for the first time, Sarah Jane leaped up from the sofa and rushed across to the Doctor. 'But how do we find this Zor, Doctor? How do we know if he was part of the Pescaton migration?'

The Doctor smiled wryly. 'Believe me, Sarah Jane, Zor's around – somewhere.'

'That's all very well.' Now the Professor came across to join them. 'But he could be anywhere around the world, from Times Square to Timbuktoo.'

'No, Bud, I don't think so.' The Doctor was becoming restless; he moved around the Observatory Hall without settling in any particular part of it. It was a sign Sarah Jane recognized only too well. 'I know this may sound somewhat immodest, but I happen to think that it's me Zor is after.'

Sarah Jane and the Professor exchanged a startled look.

'You see, Zor is hungry for knowledge,' the Doctor called back from the steps up to the observation platform. 'And I happen to have the kind of knowledge he needs.'

'But how do you know this, Doctor?' Sarah Jane called back to him. 'How can you be so sure?'

'I was sure from the moment I met young Martin. When I saw the look in his eyes, I knew at once that Zor was using the boy as a point of communication between him and me. That could only be achieved through someone with a high IQ.' The Doctor's voice echoed throughout the hall below and around the glass dome above. 'There's no doubt in my mind whatsoever,' he boomed. 'Find Zor, and we'll destroy the entire Pescaton race forever!'

At the Thames Estuary, the Army opened fire on the Pescatons as more than a dozen of the creatures emerged from the water and ran amok along the adjoining residential areas of Westcliff, Southend and Shoeburyness. But no weapons could bring down the invaders, no bullets or bombs could penetrate the steely scales of their massive bodies. The Pescatons, it seemed, were invincible.

At Canvey Island, the creatures roared, hissed, and growled their way into bungalows on a huge estate, and attacked terrified people unable to get away from them fast enough. And if anyone dared to challenge the rampaging beasts, they were snatched and devoured within seconds.

Further along the coast, at the ECPU Base Headquarters, there was frenzied activity as Mike Ridgewell and his team struggled to plot the path of the invaders who were now gaining a foothold on the coastal regions, destroying everything as they went.

'It's extraordinary,' exclaimed Helen Briggs, who was at a computer, charting the exact direction of the Pescaton thrust inland. The monitor screen was displaying a whole patchwork of lines, obviously part of a well-planned strategy like any other military campaign. 'The creatures seem to be consolidating their positions on this side of the Estuary. They haven't yet made a move into Kent.'

'Give them time!' Mike was on the telephone, trying without success to get through to his chiefs at the Department of the Environment in London. 'Damn the lines!' he snapped, slamming down the receiver.

'Mike!' called Helen, excitedly. 'Come and take a look at this!'

Mike hurried across to Helen, where information was just being flashed on to her monitor via the main Home Office and Defence Ministry computer network. A white flash read: *01.04 HOURS. R.N. DESTROYER UNDER ATTACK FROM ALIEN CREATURE KENT SIDE OF ESTUARY. RESISTING.* 'I knew that would happen, sooner or later,' said Helen. But no sooner had she tapped her 'Information Received' key, than another white flash appeared on the screen. This one read: *GENERAL FLOOD ALERT! THAMES LEVEL UP 14 METRES. CONSIDERABLE OVERFLOW LONDON DOCKLANDS, GREENWICH, RICHMOND, AND WINDSOR.*

Helen and Mike exchanged grim looks.

'It's getting serious, Mike. How long can we hold on?'

Mike had no time to answer, for one of his men burst into the office, breathless and near frantic. 'Creatures on the cliffs, Mike! Three of them – no more than three or four minutes from the perimeter fence!'

Mike and Helen rushed to the window overlooking the cliffs and sea. Through binoculars, they immediately caught a glimpse of three massive Pescatons lumbering their way across the clifftops, heading straight towards the ECPU compound.

'My God,' said Helen. 'Just look at them.' She fell back from the window in terror. This was the first time she had seen one of the creatures since her near fatal underwater encounter with them on the bed of the Estuary.

'Get everybody in here, and turn off the lights!' Mike was suddenly busy and yelling out orders at the top of his voice.

The entire building was now bursting with activity, as ECPU personnel rushed from one room to another, some of them trying to make contact with the police and military, and others rather pointlessly slamming doors and windows. 'What about the perimeter lights, Mike?' somebody called.

'No! Leave them on! Let's keep an eye on the –'

No one could understand why he had stopped short of calling the creatures what he really thought of them.

The building was plunged into darkness.

Central London was now in the grip of a full-scale Pescaton onslaught. From the top of the Post Office Tower the creatures could be seen quite clearly, rampaging through one street after another, smashing everything in their path. It was an incredible sight, for the great sprawling creatures seemed to move as one, as though controlled by an outside force. The crowds who watched them thought they resembled the worst of the football hooligans who did practically the same thing every Saturday afternoon. At least the Pescatons did not claim to be human.

Thanks to the frenzied Pescaton activity in the river, the Thames was now flooding its banks right through London and out towards the Berkshire countryside. People fled for their lives, for their fate was either to be drowned or to be eaten alive by horrific alien creatures. Even the House of Commons had been evacuated, after the Members' Terrace had been virtually destroyed. The House of Lords, however, refused to adjourn. Their Lordships never allowed themselves to be intimidated by anyone.

Old Ben had taken cover in his usual nightly haunt, Hyde Park. As he trundled his way towards his favourite bench down near the Serpentine, he tried to ignore the fires that were burning all around him. From Marble Arch to the north to Victoria and Westminster in the south, the whole sky above was glowing red, and the air was pierced with the wailing sound of police cars and ambulances and the endless ringing of fire engine bells.

When the old boy eventually reached his bench, he put down the sleeping bag that he had stolen from Tommy and sorted through his carrier bag which contained bits and pieces of food and cigarette ends that he had cadged during the day. However, when he was about to make up his bed for the night, he discovered that his bench was covered with a sticky green slime. Grunting his disapproval, he picked up his things, moved to the next bench, and, draining the last drop of rum from a small bottle donated to him by a generous American tourist, quickly settled down for the night.

About five minutes later, his eyes suddenly sprang open. It wasn't that he had actually heard anything strange, for the night was still dominated by the sound of shouts and emergency services tearing to and fro around the park. But there was something. The law, he thought, coming to pick him up for loitering for the umpteenth time. He sat up quickly and looked back into the Park. No 'flatfoots'.

But when he turned around towards the Serpentine, his eyes widened with horror and disbelief. Drifting over the whole surface of the water was a green ethereal haze, faint just then, but gradually growing in colour and intensity. For a few moments, old Ben just stared, almost hypnotized by the sheer beauty of the spectacle. To him, it seemed as though the lake was haunted, and that he would suddenly see a ghostly figure rise up from the depths.

He snapped out of his trance, and rubbed his eyes. He picked up the empty rum bottle that he had just discarded, shook it, and looked at the label, just to assure himself that he was not drunk. With a shrug of the shoulders, he threw the bottle down on to the grass. But just as he had settled down again, he was shaken by a very different sound.

Sitting up with a start and looking out towards the lake, he saw two Pescatons rearing up out of the water through the green haze, roaring and hissing, struggling to get a foothold on the concrete footpath.

In a flash, old Ben had abandoned all his worldly possessions, and was fleeing for his life back towards the main road. Not really knowing which way he was running in the dark, he suddenly tripped over, landing flat on his face on the grass.

'Got you!'

The old boy yelled out in terror and refused to look up.

'Come on now, Ben!' The voice sounded vaguely familiar. 'No need to be frightened.'

Ben looked up, and in the dim light from a nearby park lamp, he could see the Doctor and Sarah Jane. But he was still shaking with terror. 'Gotta get outa here! They're after me! Them things – they're after me, I tell yer!'

'What things, Ben?' asked Sarah Jane, urgently. 'D'you mean the Pescatons?'

The old boy merely shivered with fear.

The Doctor persisted. 'Are they in the park, Ben? Tell me, please. Are they?'

Unable to utter another word, Ben got up quickly and rushed off.

'Ben!' Sarah Jane yelled. But it was no use. The old boy had already disappeared.

'Let's go!' The Doctor was already racing off towards the Serpentine.

'No, Doctor! This is madness!' Even in the dim light, the Doctor could see Sarah Jane's pale white face. 'We can't go down to that lake. We musn't! Don't you understand? This time we'll be killed if those creatures catch up with us.'

'I must find Zor, Sarah Jane. It's the only way to put an end to this nightmare.'

'But if it really is you he's after, he'll do everything in his power to destroy you!'

Although he couldn't actually see the expression on her face, the Doctor talked straight at her. 'Sarah Jane. If I don't find Zor, he'll destroy all of us.'

They reached the lake. The green haze had disappeared, and the surface of the water was calm and serene again. But the Doctor knew only too well what had been going on there. During all his travels through time and space, he had learnt how to detect a 'presence', whether it was physical or super-natural.

For a few minutes, they walked cautiously in the dark along the paved footpath at the side of the lake. The sound they made was a curious one, for, despite the fact that they were in a large open park, their footsteps seemed to echo. As they made their way to the bridge which crossed the Serpentine, the Doctor came to a sudden halt and listened intently. It was at times like this that Sarah Jane never interrupted him, for she knew that the Doctor needed all his powers of concentration, which were an essential part of his unique powers and far superior to those of anyone on Earth. In a flash, he was gone. 'This way!' he called. 'Hurry, Sarah Jane!'

Once again Sarah Jane did her best to catch up with him. When she did, she saw for the first time what he had heard. It was a horrifying but fascinating sight. In a clearing on the Kensington side of the Park, two Pescaton creatures were hard at work, erecting a cluster of cones made out of their own green slime. Careful not to be seen, the Doctor led Sarah Jane into a secluded position where they could get a better view, and for several minutes they stood there, marvelling at the extraordinary skill with which the creatures erected their hideous structures. The slime itself was a substance that was emitted from the creature's mouth, rather like that of a prehistoric monster. But it was the way the structure was erected that both intrigued and revolted the Doctor, for the cones were built up layer by layer until they formed an apex. In some mysterious way, it all looked quite beautiful.

Although they were well hidden behind one of the Park's huge oak trees, the Doctor and Sarah Jane were surprised when the creatures suddenly stopped what they were doing, and after a brief hesitation, turned in unison to look at them.

'They've seen us, Doctor,' whispered Sarah Jane anxiously. 'We've got to get away from here.'

'Yes, I know,' replied the Doctor strangely. He was still watching the creatures. 'Leave me, Sarah Jane. I'll be perfectly all right.'

Sarah Jane panicked. 'No, Doctor! I'm not going without you!'

The Doctor turned and snapped back at her. 'Do as I say, Sarah Jane! Get back to the Professor as fast as you can. Tell him – tell him I intend to find Zor.'

As the Doctor spoke, the two Pescatons started to lumber menacingly towards them.

'Doctor!' Sarah Jane backed away, horrified by the creature's advance. 'Please, Doctor! I don't want to leave you!'

The Doctor shouted at her above the roar and hiss of the creatures. 'Run, Sarah Jane! Run...!'

Sarah Jane knew it was useless to argue with the Doctor. Reluctantly she left him behind and ran as fast as she could back to the bridge, and out to the main road.

It was the last she would see of the Doctor for some time.

Mike, Helen and the rest of the team crouched in the darkened ECPU building, waiting for the first approach of the three Pescatons who were rapidly approaching the perimeter fence outside.

'What time is it now, Helen?' whispered Mike, his eyes just peering through the drawn Venetian blinds.

'That's the fourth time you've asked me that in the last fifteen minutes.' Helen exhaled smoke from her cigarette, and looked at her watch. 'It's just coming up to one-thirty.'

Mike sighed. 'Damn it! Still another four hours to go before sunup. I hope to God we can hold out till then.'

'Mike!' Pete called from a window on the other side of the room. 'I can see them!'

Mike and Helen quickly raised their binoculars and peered out. 'Oh my God,' exclaimed Helen.

The three massive Pescatons reached the wire perimeter fence on the edge of the compound. For a moment, they stood there, roaring and hissing, their giant shadows stretching almost to the ECPU building itself. But just when it seemed that they would tear down the fence as though it were a piece of paper, they hesitated, and suddenly became very fraught and disoriented.

'What's the matter with them?' called Mike. 'Why have they stopped?'

'It's the light,' said Helen, focusing her binoculars on the creatures. 'They're angry with the light.'

107

'They're turning back!' called Pete. 'It's too much for them. They can't take it!'

At the perimeter fence, the creatures roared louder than ever before as they slowly backed away and tried to shield their eyes from the compound floodlighting.

Inside the ECPU building, a loud triumphant cheer went up from all the team.

The floodlighting went out. The entire place was plunged into darkness again.

'For God's sake! What's going on?' yelled Mike.

'It's the generator, Mike,' someone yelled back gloomily. 'It's broken down again.'

In the silence that followed, there was an air of desperation and pessimism. From the perimeter fence, there was no sound from the creatures.

No sound at all.

They crouched in the dark, and waited to see what the Pescatons' next move would be.

They did not have to wait long.

10

THE DEADLY ENCOUNTER

London was in the firm grip of a mass attack. All along the
Thames the grotesque creatures were emerging, one after the
other, from the river. As night wore on, the streets, thorough-
fares, and even the majestic dome of St Paul's were echoing
to the deafening Pescaton roar; no one was given the chance
to sleep. Further upriver, one of the creatures even managed
to reach the grassy outer slopes of Windsor Castle. It was
reported later that the Royal occupant, who happened to be
in residence at the time, was 'not amused'.

In the opposite direction, downriver, on the mouth of the
Estuary, Mike, Helen and their team crouched in the ECPU
base in the dark, feeling utterly helpless as they waited for
the aggressive creatures to start their attack. The tension
finally reached a climax when the silence was suddenly
pierced by the roar and hissing of the creatures and the distant
sound of the compound perimeter fence being smashed to
pieces.

'We've got to get some light out there!' yelled Mike. 'How
much longer do we have to wait for that generator?'

'Joe and Pete are out there working on it, Mike! They need
another five or ten minutes,' a voice called from the darkness.

'Five or ten minutes!' This time it was Helen's desperate voice. 'We could all be eaten alive by then!'

'Not that the light's going to make much difference,' said Mike, using his binoculars to peer through the window. 'But it might confuse them for a while. If we could just make it till daybreak.'

'Not a hope!' Helen switched on her torch to check her wrist-watch. 'There's at least another three or four hours before sunrise.'

Another man's voice called from the other side of the darkened room. 'How do we know these things'll give up when it's daylight?'

'We don't,' Mike said over his shoulder. 'But the Doctor says they can only survive in the dark. That means they'd have to try to make it back to the river.'

'Mike – look!' Helen shone her torch through a crack in the Venetian blinds over the windows.

Mike immediately focused his binoculars through the window. The three Pescatons had torn down the perimeter fence, and in a flood of their own dazzling green light were slowly heading towards the ECPU building. Mike and his team watched the creatures approach in horror and astonishment. They were raised up to their full height, clawed hands striking out at the night air as they moved, their needlelike teeth glistening with anticipation. To Mike and Helen they seemed like giant gargoyles, a manifestation of the Devil himself. But although their movements were erratic and clumsy, they seemed to move in unison, as though functioning through the same brain. And they were using their flat nostrils to sniff out their prey, like animals searching for food.

'They're coming straight for us,' said Mike, gloomily, half to himself. 'If we don't get that generator working, we haven't a hope.'

Even as he spoke, the three Pescatons were lumbering towards a large brick hut in the grounds of the compound. Inside, Joe and Pete were working frantically to repair the electrical generator.

In Hyde Park, the Doctor was having his own problems with the Pescatons. For nearly an hour he had played a cat-and-mouse game with them, dodging behind trees, outflanking them, always just managing to keep his distance. For during this confrontation he had discovered one important element of the Pescatons' behaviour which proved useful to him. Their movements were not only cumbersome, but they seemed to have no cohesion. At times they lumbered towards him as though they were blind, which gave him the opportunity to avoid their stretched-out claws. But just when he thought it was safe to approach them closer, they would suddenly fix the green laserlike beam from their eyes on him, which momentarily stunned his brain and sent him reeling over and over along the ground. On each occasion so far the Doctor was able to recover himself just in time, but the pulverizing mental attack emanating from the creatures was intense. Once again, it was only the Doctor's own special powers which had resisted those of Zor, leader of the Pescatons.

However, it was clearly not the Doctor's life that Zor wanted. After all, time and again the Creatures had had the opportunity to kill him, but at the last moment they had always held back. But how, the Doctor wondered, would he find Zor? For if he wasn't found soon, Earth would surely come under the complete domination of the voracious Pescaton species. But where to look? Zor could be anywhere in the whole world – perhaps in that very park itself. It was an impossible task, like trying to find a needle in a haystack. Or was it? Was it conceivable that Zor's bizarre family of fish-creatures could lead the Doctor to their Leader? And if so, how?

The answer came sooner than the Doctor expected.

'Doctor!' An exact replica of the Doctor's own voice boomed out of nowhere. It was a chilling sound.

The Doctor swung round with a start. 'Who's there?' He could see nothing in the darkness behind him.

'Doctor!'

The Doctor turned back quickly, to find that the two

111

creatures who had been lumbering towards him had suddenly become static, almost like statues – not a twitch, hiss, roar, or movement of any kind from them. He looked from one to the other, highly suspicious. 'Zor?' he called, weakly. But as his confidence rose, so did his voice. 'Is that you, Zor?'

Zor's voice came back at him in the Doctor's own tones, slow, but loud and resonant, echoing throughout the trees. 'I am waiting for you, Doctor. We have much to talk about.'

'Where are you?' The Doctor looked all around him. It was as though he could only hear the voice inside his own mind. 'Why can't I see you?'

Zor hesitated briefly. 'I am waiting for you, Doctor. Follow me.'

'How can I follow you if I can't see you?'

But suddenly, the Doctor could see Zor. Not in the darkness of the park, but in the dark side of the Doctor's own mind. Even though his eyes were wide open, he could see Zor, spread out before him like a vast lump of ancient carved rock, protected by the dark night of the tunnel.

Tunnel? What tunnel?

The Doctor tried to identify the location inside his own mind. It was all shaped so methodically, so carefully. Wires, and rails shining at his feet as he walked.

Tunnel? What tunnel?

His own subconscious kept asking the same question over and over again. 'Where ... am ... I?'

As the Doctor's voice reverberated around the trees, a new and more terrifying sound snapped him out of his telepathic trance. It was a cracking and squealing sound, which overwhelmed the night air, forcing the Doctor to cover his ears in pain. The Doctor felt as though thousands of mice were scrambling around his feet. But what he saw were not mice, for the green slime cones were cracking open one by one, and out of them rushed the newly hatched young of the Pescatons. Dozens of them, screeching, hissing, squealing, rushing past the Doctor, all heading towards the Serpentine, where they leapt in with loud splashes and quickly disappeared beneath the surface. And following closely after

112

them were their elders, now fully restored to their ugly lumbering state of mobility.

The Doctor walked across to the lake, which was soon quiet and calm again. But he knew only too well that beneath the surface Zor's family was increasing at an ever alarming rate.

'Joe! Pete! Get the hell out of there!' Just a few yards away, the three Pescatons were gradually closing in on the generator hut where two of his men were desperately struggling to restore the exterior floodlighting.

'We're nearly there, Mike,' called Pete from inside the hut. 'Give us another minute. We're nearly there.'

The creatures roared in unison.

'Get out of there – both of you! That's an order!'

The creatures were within a few feet of the generator hut.

Helen sprang to her feet. 'We can't just sit here! We've got to stop those damned things somehow!'

Mike turned to find her rushing out of the office. 'Helen! Where're you going? Get back here!'

Helen was already in the outer office collecting the warning flash pistol from the emergency cupboard. But by the time Mike reached her she had rushed out into the grounds of the compound. 'Helen!' he yelled. 'You can't do anything with those things! Don't be stupid! Get back here!'

Ignoring Mike's frenzied calls, Helen rushed across the grounds of the compound, and headed straight towards the three Pescatons who were now bearing down on the generator hut. As she went she quickly loaded a cartridge shell into the pistol, then moved in as close as she could to the first creature.

'No Helen!' Mike was runnning towards her from the ECPU building. 'Don't do it!'

All three creatures were suddenly distracted from tearing down the generator hut, and in unison, turned their attention towards Helen.

Helen took aim with the warning pistol, then fired a shot straight at one of the creatures. To a deafening roar from all three, a massive orange flame burst out of one of them.

113

Convinced that she had destroyed her target, Helen quickly started to reload her pistol. But to her horror, her first creature 'target' extinguished the orange flame stuck in its neck, and all three continued to bear down on her. In absolute terror, Helen turned to run. But she was too late, for all three creatures used their eyes to direct the green laser-like beams at her.

Mike threw himself at her, and brought them both to the ground. Shielding her with his own body, he waited for the fearful moment.

The Pescatons towered over them, roaring and hissing, ready for the final aggressive strike.

A grinding sound was heard from the generator hut, and suddenly the entire compound was bathed in light.

From the inside the ECPU building there came a roar of cheers and triumphant yells. Mike turned to look up at the creatures, who were in a state of total bewilderment and disorientation. They screeched, and squealed, and roared, and hissed, their claws reaching out aimlessly towards the night sky. But Mike knew only too well that their state of confusion was only temporary. 'Quick, Helen!' he said urgently, pulling her up and supporting her with his arms. 'Let's get the hell out of here.'

Helen was too dazed from the attack to do anything but allow Mike to drag her back to the safety of the ECPU building.

For a few moments, the three Pescatons lumbered around helplessly in the dazzling floodlights before finally retreating into the darkness beyond the compound perimeter.

Mike prayed for only one thing.

Daylight.

By the time the Doctor had got back to the Observatory on Highgate Hill, the sun had well and truly risen over Hampstead Heath. Despite the constant wail of police and ambulance sirens, and the smell of burning buildings which was drifting over the rooftops of London in the far distance, the dawn chorus of wild birds continued as though it was a day like any other.

After his exhausting night out on Hampstead Heath, Professor Emmerson was not looking his usual ebullient self. Just for once, he had given up peering through his telescope and was at the window taking in the vast panorama of London rooftops, many of which were still smouldering after the night's Pescaton attack. 'Haven't seen a sight like that since the Blitz,' he said, gloomily, hands in pockets, and still sucking his unlit pipe. 'It's a funny thing, isn't it, Doctor? All these years I've been staring up at the sky, and yet never once did I think of it as a threat. Perhaps its just as well people like me don't really know what's waiting up there for us in space.' It was the most serious thing the Professor had said for a long time. But he meant it, for, despite all his eccentric ways, he loved the planet that he was born and bred on, and was depressed that so many of his fellow human beings took it so much for granted.

The Doctor joined him at the window and patted him affectionately on the back. 'What news of the Pescatons?' he said softly.

'The television says they've all gone back into either the river or the sea. I hope they damned well stay there!'

The Doctor sighed, and shook his head anxiously. 'That's most unlikely, I'm afraid.'

'But what are we going to do about these – these fish-devils!' The Professor was more like his old self again, angrily thumping his fist against the window frame. 'If we don't do something about them soon, they'll wipe out the whole human race!' He stopped looking out of the window, and returned to his desk in the hall below. 'We can't even save young Martin Wilson's life,' he snapped, pouring himself a cup of tea from a vacuum flask. 'They've got half the Metropolitan Police out on the Heath, and they still can't break into that cone!'

The Doctor turned with a start. 'What did you say, Bud?' He rushed down to join the Professor in the hall. 'The police are trying to break into the Pescaton cones?'

'So I've heard.'

'But this is madness! They could be releasing a whole new batch of young creatures. They must be left where they are!'

The Professor sipped his hot tea, burning his lips. 'And what about young Martin? Do we just leave him where he is?'

The Doctor was getting agitated. 'Bud,' he almost snapped. 'We don't even know that Martin is inside that cone.'

'But what if he is?'

The Doctor thought carefully before answering. 'He'll be saved.' And exchanging a measured glance with his old friend, continued, 'I give you my promise.'

The Professor smiled, poured another cup of tea from the flask, and offered it to the Doctor.

The Doctor smiled back, and took the tea. 'By the way, where's Sarah Jane?'

'Oh, she had a shower, and left soon after it was light.' For the first time, the Professor actually lit his pipe and blew out a cloud of smoke. 'I think she said she was going to try and look up one of her old workmates in Fleet Street. Something about writing up a story on you.'

'Me!' The Doctor laughed. 'She'll have a hard time. Nobody will believe a word.' Then he added, with a wry smile to himself, 'They never do.'

The Professor took his tea and went to sit at his computer. 'By all accounts, she'll have a difficult time getting around. Apparently they've stopped all the buses, so it'll be hell getting a taxi.' He started tapping away at the computer keys. 'Anyway, she said she'd probably take the tube.'

The Doctor's eyes flicked up immediately, but he did not turn around to look at the Professor. 'The tube?' He had a strange, vacant look on his face.

'The tube! Come on now, old chap. Don't tell me you've never travelled on a London Underground train before?' He swivelled around on his chair to wait for his friend's reply.

The Doctor had gone.

Sarah Jane thought it seemed ages since she last travelled on an Underground train. Usually she preferred to travel by bus, but the streets of London were always so jammed with traffic

116

that the tube was the only way to get somewhere on time. Unfortunately on most days, the trains were crammed with rush-hour commuters, and it was hardly ever possible to claim a standing position let alone a seat. This morning, however, things were very different. After the overnight Pescaton invasion of the city, the streets were practically deserted, with no buses or taxis and very few cars. As for the Underground trains, they carried hardly any passengers at all.

Sarah Jane found it all very eerie, as she made her way along deserted passages to the empty platforms. As she waited for her Piccadilly Line train to appear, two mischievous mice ran unmolested along the side of the electrified rail, collecting every crumb of litter they could find. When the train finally arrived, Sarah Jane discovered that her only fellow passengers were a large man in a pinstriped suit and trilby hat, and a young punky-looking girl with spiked hair, who was gently rocking her baby to sleep in its pushchair.

Sarah Jane changed trains at Holborn, for, as she was making her way to Fleet Street, she decided to change on to the small branch line to the Aldwych. On normal working days, Holborn was one of the busiest stations on the London Underground network, where most people alighted for their jobs in the nearby City and West End of London. Today, however, the escalators were clear for anyone to use.

A few minutes later, Sarah Jane felt decidedly uneasy when she discovered that she was the only passenger in the first compartment of her Aldwych-bound train. However, as it was only one stop, she took a deep breath, sat down in a seat near the automatic doors and waited patiently for the train to reach its destination. The two or three minute journey seemed much longer than it actually was, for the train, which was covered with graffiti inside as well as outside, was ancient and rattled noisily. Finally, however, the train pulled into Aldwych Station, so Sarah Jane leapt to her feet, stood in front of the doors, and waited anxiously for them to open.

They remained closed. After two minutes she became nervous, for the platform was deserted, and there was no sign of any station staff. When another two minutes passed, she started banging on the door window.

'Hey! What's going on! Open these doors!' But the doors remained very firmly closed. No one appeared. In desperation, she grabbed hold of the emergency handle on the train ceiling, and pulled it hard.

The lights went out, plunging both train and platform into darkness. 'Oh no!' Sarah Jane's voice sounded hollow in the dark, as though she was being smothered by a pillow. She began to panic and she banged with both fists on the door. 'Where... is... everybody! Let... me... out... of... here!' she screeched.

Suddenly, her yells for help were completely overwhelmed by the train itself, which started vibrating and rocking from side to side. Sarah Jane screamed for all she was worth. She was living through a nightmare. And then, when the train stopped vibrating and rocking, she was subjected to an even more horrific experience. Gradually, light was beginning to filter through the compartment windows, only dimly at first, then building to a dazzling glare which cast sinister shadows across the rows of empty seats.

But the light did not originate in the Underground generators.

The entire train and platform were now engulfed in a flood of emerald-green fluorescent light...

With little or no transport available, the Doctor ran through the streets of North London. Luckily his long legs were a great advantage, for it took him very little time to find the nearest tube station at Highgate. When he got there, however, he had no idea where to go. 'Please!' he begged a Jamaican ticket collector. 'Are there hold-ups on any of the Underground lines this morning?'

The ticket collector took off his cap and scratched his head. 'Nothing, man. Mind you, it don't make no difference, 'cause we ain't got no passengers!' He roared with laughter and withdrew into his ticket collector's cabin.

The Doctor had no time to ask any more questions, so he rushed past the ticket barrier, and started to make his way down the escalator. He had not even reached halfway, when the voice of the ticket collector boomed out to him from the top of the escalator. 'If you goin' to the Aldwych, man, forget it! Sound like one of the dem fish things got stuck down there!'

The last thing the Doctor heard as he leaped off the last escalator step was a deep-throated laugh echoing around the curved Undergound arches.

It took the Doctor no more than fifteen minutes to get to King's Cross, where he quickly changed onto the Piccadilly Line for Holborn. But when he eventually reached Holborn and tried to make for the Aldwych Branch Line, he was astonished to find his way barred by a hoard of armed Special Police Constables.

'I'm sorry, sir,' said a burly Police Superintendent who was wearing a bulletproof jerkin as though he was protecting himself against armed terrorists. 'Aldwych Line's closed today.'

The Doctor tried to get a look at the platform over the Superintendent's shoulder, but without success. 'What's happening?' he asked. 'What's going on?'

'The tunnel's blocked, sir. We've had to turn off the electric current on the line.'

'Blocked? Blocked by what?'

The Superintendent grinned briefly at one of his team. 'Come now, sir,' he grunted, clearing his throat. 'It can hardly have escaped your notice what's been going on in London all through the night... Hey!'

Before the Superintendent could say another word, the Doctor had pushed past him, sprinting towards the platform. To the accompaniment of shouts and whistles, and half the Special Police team chasing after him, the Doctor leapt on to the rail lines, and scuttled off into the tunnel in the direction of the Aldwych.

The torch beams from the police team following the Doctor gradually disappeared. No one, it appears, was willing to throw caution to the wind and walk straight into the claws of the Pescatons. The Doctor, however, moved with great skill, as he found his way on to the tunnel ledge, and used the palms of his hands to feel along the dust-covered wires and walls. It was a perilous journey, for he had no torch to pierce the menacing dark which was now engulfing him. Behind him, in the distance, he could still hear the yelling voices of the Special Police team, but after a while, even those sounds became inaudible as the Doctor ploughed further into the eerie silence.

Twenty minutes later, the darkness ahead gradually became a dazzling green glow, and the Doctor got his first view of the tail end of the train stuck on the Aldwych platform. Just as he reached the end of the platform itself, he decided to pause and take a good look at the train. So for a few moments, he accustomed himself to the green glare, before cautiously moving down the platform, peering into each compartment as he went. When he reached about halfway, he suddenly heard a distraught female voice calling from inside the train.

'Let me out of here! I can't bear this any longer! Please – don't leave me here!' It was Sarah Jane's voice.

The Doctor suddenly broke into a trot, checking each compartment as he went. 'Sarah Jane! Is that you? Where are you?' he called.

'Doctor! Here, Doctor! At the front of the train!'

'Sarah Jane!'

The Doctor finally found her, trapped inside the front compartment, her face pressed up against the window of the automatic door, distorted in the ghastly green light which was now flooding the entire tunnel. 'Get me out of here, Doctor!' Her frantic voice was muffled. 'Get me out!'

The Doctor looked around quickly for something with which he could use to break down the compartment door. But there was nothing. In desperation, he went to the driver's cabin. To his great surprise, the door was not locked. Cautiously opening the door, the first thing he saw was the driver, totally immobilized, like a statue, propped up at his steering controls, staring through the train's windscreen, his face flooded with the dazzling green light. The Doctor turned to look through the windscreen.

'We meet again, Doctor.' It was Zor's voice, booming out in the Doctor's tones again from the tunnel dead ahead.

The Doctor stared in awe and horror at the massive shape of the leader of the Pescatons, whose ghastly form was spread out over the walls and ceilings of the tunnel like a huge spider in its web.

They were together again – the Doctor and his most voracious foe, a deadly encounter that was inevitable ever since the Doctor escaped from the planet of Pesca.

'We meet again.' Zor's voice seemed to pierce right through the Doctor's brain. 'For the last time, Doctor.'

The Doctor shielded his eyes. 'Your power is broken, Zor!' he called back with as firm a voice as he could manage. 'The Pescaton civilization is at an end.'

As he spoke, Zor's body seemed to inflate to fill every conceivable space around it in the tunnel. 'You are wrong, Doctor. This is no end for the Pescatons. It is only the beginning.'

Zor's voice was gradually seeping through to the Doctor's mind, and he felt all his resistance draining away. Zor's powerful computer brain was virtually eating the Doctor alive, extracting his knowledge like a huge magnet. But, as on so many previous occasions throughout his travels in time and space, the Doctor had that special reserve of power in the corner of his own brain that could never be taken from him. The Doctor had 'seen' for himself how Zor and the entire Pescaton species could be destroyed. Zor's great protector was the darkness itself.

If the leader of the Pescatons could not be persuaded to leave the tunnel and go into the sunlight, then the sunlight should be brought to him.

Detaching himself from Zor's mental onslaught the Doctor rushed out of the driver's cabin, and to Sarah Jane's surprise and horror, left the platform and hurried off through the exit.

'Doctor!' Sarah Jane's pleas for help went unheard. Completely exhausted, she flopped back on one of the many empty compartment seats, convinced that the Doctor had been forced to leave her to a horrifying fate.

By the time the Doctor returned, the train was rocking and vibrating to Zor's command. Inside the compartment, Sarah Jane felt her life ebbing away beneath the force of the Pescaton power, and she slumped on to the floor in a faint before she had the chance to see what the Doctor was doing.

With the help of two or three young policemen he had managed to recruit, the Doctor was erecting three huge ultraviolet arc lamps along the front section of the platform. 'Keep them all directed towards the front carriage!' he yelled. 'Fast as you can, now!'

The lamps were quickly put in place, but just as the young police constables were trying to connect the wires to the platform electricity supply, each of them in turn was overcome by the haze of Zor's mental control which pervaded along the entire platform. Unperturbed, the Doctor continued connecting the wires himself.

'Doctor!' Zor's voice boomed out from the tunnel. 'Only the beginning, Doctor! The beginning!'

'That's what you think, my friend,' the Doctor yelled back, then rushed out to the generator box just outside in the exit passage. But as he was about to plug in to the station's emergency power system, Zor's energy succeeded in causing the plug to blow out of the switch with a bright blue flame. The force of the blowout knocked the Doctor off his feet, but he quickly recovered and inserted the plug back into the power supply.

'Kill! Kill! Kill!' Zor's voice thundered and echoed around the tunnels, and the train, walls and platform vibrated.

'You've killed for the last time, Zor!' The Doctor shouted. 'You had your chance. You destroyed your own planet. But you won't destroy this one!' He pressed the power button, and immediately, the three huge arc lights burst into activity. Zor's booming, menacing voice immediately deteriorated into a roar, then a hiss, then an immense squeal as the dazzling green glare began to fade until it was finally eliminated altogether. During all this, the Doctor shielded his eyes, but when the train and platform lights suddenly came on again, he rushed straight back to the train, where the automatic doors were just opening.

'What's going on out here?' complained the train driver, who emerged from his cabin, seemingly unaware of his enforced state of immobility. 'There's a fine for pulling that emergency handle, y'know!'

The Doctor came out from the carriage, carrying Sarah Jane in his arms. Then, as he put her gently down on to the platform, he called to the driver, 'Get that train out of here – fast as you can!'

The driver, bewildered by the extraordinary scene all around him on the platform, did what he was told and a few moments later, the train was reversing at speed out of the station, heading back towards Holborn.

The Doctor left Sarah Jane for a moment, and climbed back down on to the tracks again. In the tunnel just ahead of him, was Zor, leader of the Pescatons, now a steaming mass of green slime like a huge green iceberg thawing in the midday sun.

'Kill! Kill! Kill!' Zor hardly had the strength to be heard.

'Yes, yes,' replied the Doctor, without a shred of compassion. Then, in what might have been either a strange act of defiance, or a jubilant moment of celebration, he took his flute from his inside jacket pocket and started to play. As he did so, he watched Zor's body slowly disintegrate. By the time he had finished playing, all that was left of the Pescaton leader was a small heap of green powder which would eventually disperse during the arrival of the next train.

Later in the day, the Doctor and Sarah Jane arrived back at ECPU Headquarters where they heard the news from all parts of the world that the Pescaton creatures had suffered the same fate as Zor himself. For what seemed to be no reason at all, their bodies had simply disintegrated, their cones cracked open, and any young still waiting to be hatched were transformed into a heap of green powder.

'I don't know who you are, Doctor,' said Mike, as he and Helen bid the Doctor and Sarah Jane farewell on the beach, 'but if you see any more Pescatons on your travels, please tell them to find somewhere else to settle.'

The Doctor laughed. Then, after he and Sarah Jane had shook hands with Mike and Helen, they made their way along the beach back to the TARDIS.

The sun was dipping low on the horizon out at sea, and the Estuary looked more serene and beautiful than ever before.

Sarah Jane was horrified to see two young boys swimming in the water just offshore near the beach huts. 'Are they mad!' she spluttered. 'Suppose there are still any of those things in the water out there?'

The Doctor smiled, and put a reassuring arm around her shoulder. 'Don't worry,' he replied. 'No chance of that.'

Sarah Jane looked up at him. 'Positive?'

'Positive.'

A few minutes later they had reached the TARDIS. To Sarah Jane's relief, the shell of solid green slime had dropped away and its powder could be seen amongst the sand and shingle on the beach.

After a last quick look around, the Doctor opened the TARDIS door for Sarah Jane to enter first. Just as she did so, however, the air was pierced by a terrifying squealing sound, as three young Pescaton creatures suddenly shot out of the TARDIS, and straight past Sarah Jane.

She screamed, and threw herself into the Doctor's arms.

But as they stood in the doorway of the TARDIS and watched, the three young creatures immediately found themselves subjected to the sun's rays, and within seconds, they too had disintegrated.

The green powder piled up on the shingle and eventually scattered into the gentle breeze above the Thames Estuary.

On Highgate Hill, Professor Emmerson watched a small object rising up into space through his telescope. He wasn't quite sure what it was, but he had a fairly good idea. He lit his pipe and smiled to himself, lost in thoughts of time and space.